Kill Zone

ARYANNA

Lock Down Publications and Ca$h Presents
Kill Zone
A Novel by *Aryanna*

Lock Down Publications
P.O. Box 870494
Mesquite, Tx 75187

Visit our website
www.lockdownpublications.com

First Edition December 2018
Printed in the United States of America

This is a work of fiction. Names, characters, places, and incidents either are products of the author's imagination or are used fictitiously. Any similarity to actual events or locales or persons, living or dead, is entirely coincidental.

Lock Down Publications
Like our page on Facebook: Lock Down Publications
@
www.facebook.com/lockdownpublications.ldp
Cover design and layout by: **Dynasty Cover Me**
Book interior design by: **Shawn Walker**
Edited by: **Kiera Northington**

Stay Connected with Us!

Text **LOCKDOWN** to 22828 to stay up-to-date with new releases, sneak peaks, contests and more…

Submission Guideline.

Submit the first three chapters of your completed manuscript to ldpsubmissions@gmail.com, subject line: Your book's title. The manuscript must be in a .doc file and sent as an attachment. Document should be in Times New Roman, double spaced and in size 12 font. Also, provide your synopsis and full contact information. If sending multiple submissions, they must each be in a separate email.

Have a story but no way to send it electronically? You can still submit to LDP/Ca$h Presents. Send in the first three chapters, written or typed, of your completed manuscript to:

LDP: Submissions Dept
Po Box 870494
Mesquite, Tx 75187

DO NOT send original manuscript. Must be a duplicate.

Provide your synopsis and a cover letter containing your full contact information.

Thanks for considering LDP and Ca$h Presents.

Dedication

This book is dedicated to Amanda Panda Marie.

Acknowledgments

I have to thank the almighty god for continuing to guide my footsteps as well as my pen. I have to thank my soulmate and best friend for all the love, support and aggravation. Your strength is sexy but your insecurities make me love you more. Thank you for choosing me. I have to thank my littlest biggest fans the beautiful children I've been blessed with. I love you all and I thank you for touching my life with your love. I have to thank my family for being family, enough said. I have to thank my fans for still giving me a platform to showcase my talent and for appreciating what I do. I have to thank LDP family for having my back, it's all love all day. Shout out to my family and friends stuck behind the wall. I know you remain mentally strong despite the oppositions efforts to break you, and I salute that. Lastly as always, I must thank my haters for constant motivation. I love everything about you, especially my saltiness. My food taste better with salt. Lol.

ARYANNA

Chapter 1

May 2020
Norton, VA

"Hey, cutie, you gonna make some time for me later?" I looked up from the work I was doing to find Sergeant Lashonda Bishop standing next to me, smiling in the seductive way I'd become accustomed to. The beauty of her smile was matched by her five-three, one-hundred-fifty-pound frame, and the soft mocha chocolate complexion that packaged it, and I'd enjoyed every bit of it for the last six months. Nothing in prison could make you feel like you were on the street, but pussy helped in a lot of ways.

"Making time for you is always my pleasure, sweetheart, but are you sure you want to risk it?" I asked, looking around the kitchen to make sure nobody was picking up the seeds of our conversation.

"Why would you ask me that, Delontae? Ain't I *been* risking it, putting my job on the line and—"

"Slow down, Lashonda, I'm not questioning what you would do or what you have done. I only asked because today is my last day inside, which means we could spend *more* time together tomorrow and not risk your job in the process," I explained patiently.

"Oh well, I see what you're saying, but you know how you niggas be once these gates open and you've got access to new pussy and shit. You *change*, and just in case that happens, I want to remember you as you were. So, are you gonna give up the dick or what?" she asked, brazenly.

Again, I had to look around to make sure nobody was listening, because even though we were standing right in front of the ice machine, this bitch was still talking loud.

"I got you, babe. I'll be back in the unit by eight p.m. and once I take my shower, I'll meet you in our usual spot."

"I've got a better idea, why don't you wait until after nine p.m. count to take your shower and I'll meet you in there? My home girl is working your unit, so the cameras won't be a problem, and we can take our time making this last night something special," she replied, licking her lips and smiling again.

"I like how you think. Now get your sexy ass out of here before I do something in front of everybody."

Her smile only got wider as she walked away, switching her ass as hard as she could because she knew I was watching.

"I gotta hand it to you, Lion, you a bad motherfucker to have bagged that bitch. The way niggas talked about her when I first got here, I thought she *hated* inmates," Loco said, bringing me another ice bucket to fill up the antique machine with.

"I'd heard the same thing, but I ain't no inmate, I'm a convict. Plus, you already know that you don't choose in this situation, you get chosen. So, it ain't hard to tell why things worked out for me."

"Nigga, you *too* arrogant!" Loco replied, laughing.

He may have been right, but that didn't make my statement any less true, as evidenced by how aggressive Lashonda was. Even though I was only hours away from walking out of the front gates of this medium security prison, I still preferred to keep my business on the low, but apparently my sergeant boo thang didn't care. Despite what she'd said about new pussy affecting the way I treated her once I was out, I had every intention on keeping it real with her. Everything in the free world would be new to me after all the time I'd spent on the inside, so having familiar legs to slide between while I mentally adjusted seemed like the smart move. Plus, her pussy was ok.

"Keep it real, Loco. You gonna try to smash once I'm gone, ain't you?" I asked, smiling at him.

"That bitch ain't 'bout to send *me* to the box for solicitation of her fine ass! Nah playboy, that's all you. Just because I'm Mexican don't mean I like small spaces!"

His response made me laugh hard enough to spill some of the ice, but at least I knew he was being honest.

"I feel you, bruh, plus you might wanna stay on her good side, because you know I'ma make a move to reach back inside those walls," I said, giving him a knowing look.

He didn't say a word because he didn't have to. He nodded his head, dapped me up, and got back to work. It seemed like my last two hours of working in the kitchen flew by, especially with the amount of real niggas stopping through to wish me well. Of course, I caught stares from haters too, but I ignored that shit the same as I'd done countless days before this one. Weak niggas got no life out of me.

After finishing up my shit, I went around and spoke to the food stewardess I respected, before taking the short walk back to my unit up on the hill. I wanted to take a shower right away, but Lashonda was worth the wait. With my last cell mate having gone home a week earlier, I had the eight by ten cell to myself, so I should've told her to slide off in here and get dicked down. It was okay though, because I knew one of her fantasies was for me to fuck her in the shower. I just didn't figure that it would happen in the penitentiary.

With nothing to do, I kicked back and watched TV until count cleared an hour later. When my door buzzed open, I grabbed my shower bag and went to the showers at the opposite end of the tier, away from the cameras. I wasn't surprised to see Lashonda already in the control room having a conversation with her home girl, but the look on the other chick's face indicated she might not be one hundred percent with the move we were about to make. There was nothing I could say that would help, so I kept moving to our rendezvous point. Because I didn't know how long it would take to convince the CO on post to look the other way, I decided to hop in the shower and get clean for Lashonda. I hadn't been under the hot water for five minutes when the door opened and closed quickly. The only problem was that it wasn't Lashonda.

"What's on your mind, Butcher?" I asked calmly.

"You dying, nigga, what else could it be?"

I'd known Butcher for more years than I could remember so I knew he'd earned his name honestly, and the ten-inch slab of metal in his hand wasn't for show. I just didn't know why he was coming at me.

"Last time I checked, you and I didn't have a problem, so I suggest you leave the same way you came," I said, in the same calm tone.

"You're right, we don't got no smoke, but someone offered up a lot of money to see that you don't make it out alive tomorrow. It's just business."

Even though he was broad shouldered and six-one, I could still see past him to the nigga standing right outside the shower room door. I didn't know who he was, but it didn't matter. All that mattered was they'd been sent to put me down and I wasn't gonna allow that. There was no more than six feet of slick tile between us, but before he could move towards me, I reached under my pants on the bench next to me and grabbed the eight-inch piece of steel I kept on me at all times. I could tell by the way his eyes widened he didn't expect me to still be strapped, but I'd seen enough in my life to know I wasn't free until I was on the other side of the gate. Butcher's reputation preceded him, but mine preceded me as well, and now he was in a fight to the death, with a different animal than he was used to.

"What are you waiting for?" I asked, moving slowly towards him with my serrated blade out in front of me.

He didn't take any steps forward, but he didn't take any backwards either, and he never took his eyes off my knife. That was too many mistakes. When I got within lunging distance, I used my left hand to throw my soapy washcloth in his face with the speed of a MLB pitcher, knowing he would grab at it and only succeed in getting soap in his eyes. The moment that happened, he became dinner. I knocked the knife out of his hand while simultaneously ramming my blade into his groin and pushing him backwards up against the wall.

"Shut up all that damn screaming," I said, yanking the knife back out and pushing it viciously into the crease where his neck met his chin.

The way his blood sprayed onto my face made my heart hammer in my chest like I'd just done five fat-ass lines of pure Colombian cocaine, and I loved it. I stabbed him over and over in the throat until he was very much dead, and his Adam's apple was laying on the ground next to his knife. When I let his body drop, I quickly stepped out of sight beside the door and within a few seconds, the next man up stepped in. To my surprise, it was my homeboy, Loco, but the knife in his hand separated friend from foe in my mind real quick. I fired a devastating left jab that knocked him into the wall, and I followed it up with a kick to his nuts that made him forget about his knife as he vomited violently.

"I shouldn't be surprised, but I am. Somebody should've taught you that money ain't everything, my nigga," I said, sitting my knife down, and reaching down and picking up the knife belonging to the late Butcher. I pushed Loco onto his back and then straddled him.

"Wait, bruh, listen—"

His sentence was cut off by the blows I delivered to his chest. The sucking and slurping sound created by the knife ripping into his flesh gave me chills in an exciting way, but I knew I couldn't overindulge or the scene wouldn't play out right. Once he'd gargled his last breath, I quickly rinsed my bloody prints off both knives, placed one in each of their hands, and then hopped back under the water's spray to cleanse myself. When I was sure I had all the blood off me, I got dressed in a hurry, and grabbed Loco's knife on the way out. Even though I knew the cameras had to be off because of the set-up that had just gone down, I still tucked the weapon out of sight as I stalked straight towards the control room. The shock on the female CO's face told me she hadn't expected me to emerge victorious, and of course, Lashonda was nowhere to be seen.

"If you're smart, you'll let next shift discover what happened tonight. If you're dumb, you'll incriminate yourself and see how quickly Lashonda leaves you holding the bag. Now, I'm gonna go in my cell and get some rest because I have a long day tomorrow, and if my door opens before five a.m., I promise that everyone you love will die in the most painful way I can think of. Nod your head if you understand," I said calmly.

Her shaking was clearly visible through the Plexiglas that separated us, but she managed to nod slightly.

"Thank you. Have a good night. Oh, and when you see Lashonda, tell her better people than her have tried and failed. I'll let her look over her shoulder for a while, but we *will* settle up later."

ARYANNA

Chapter 2

One month later

"Mr. Mathis, Dr. Davenport will see you now."

Immediately, my attention was pulled away from my phone and given to the petite, blonde receptionist standing in front of me smiling. I had no idea when she'd come from behind her desk, or even if she'd had to call my name more than once, but I didn't like that she'd gotten right up on me unnoticed. Only a month home and my prison senses were dulling. I quickly tucked my phone into the inside pocket of my suit jacket while standing, and followed the still-smiling receptionist down the one hallway to the left of the waiting area. I could feel the nervous energy flowing through my body, which was something I hadn't felt since I'd hit my first prison yard two decades ago.

The only difference between now and then was that this doctor's visit could cause more harm than a well-placed shank. You could only die once, but this meeting was just the beginning of the end. We came to a stop at one of the two doors that lined the hallway, and after the receptionist opened it, she disappeared the way we'd come. Despite my apprehension, I walked in the room without hesitation, determined to face the part of my uncertain future like I did everything else. Like a gangsta. I'd expected to find the doctor's office unappealing in design and cold from the countless secrets kept about past patients, but I was wrong. From the plush carpeting to the Venetian blinds, the room was decorated in brown colors with gold accents, making it inviting and warm. I'd also expected to find some type of couch for patients to lay on. Instead, there were two matching, low-sitting leather chairs angled towards each other, across the glass desk from the doctor's leather swivel chair. The overall feel of the room was more consultation than treatment, and that appealed to me.

The biggest surprise though, was the doctor herself. Analyzing the room had only taken a few seconds, but my observation of her was like savoring ice-cold water, your thirst knew no limitations. Dr. Su'ryah Davenport wasn't just beautiful. She was slap an angel gorgeous! Her raven-black hair hung just above her shoulders, but it still framed her honey complexioned face in a way that was classic and sexy. I couldn't see her body's full potential because she was sitting down, but it was clear she had curves like a country back road. It was her eyes that ultimately did it for me though. It was obvious she was of mixed heritage, but her eyes were a cobalt blue I'd never seen in any black chick before. When she looked up at me, I felt my breath hit the brakes and refuse to travel any further through my body, and I was okay with that. I couldn't remember what I'd expected my doctor to look like, but it damn sure wasn't this.

"Good afternoon, Mr. Mathis, I'm Dr. Su'ryah Davenport," she said, standing and extending her hand to me.

I prayed my hesitation wasn't evident as I stepped forward to shake her hand, but being in her presence was increasing my nervousness.

"You can call me Delontae," I replied, thankful that my voice wasn't cracking.

"Okay, Delontae, you can have a seat and we'll begin. Let's start with an easy question. Do you know why you're here?"

"Yes. I did twenty years behind the wall, and the courts think I'm most likely crazy now, so I gotta see a shrink," I replied, matter-of-factly.

"Do you think you're crazy?"

"Aren't we all?" I asked, rhetorically.

My question made her smile, and a beautiful smile it was.

"To be real with you, Doc, I think everybody is a little throwed off in one way or another, but some hide it better than others do. Am I crazy? That'll be for you to judge. I'll say that I'm different," I conceded.

"I'm not here to judge you, Delontae, I'm here to help you. So, tell me what you mean when you say you're different," she said, turning her handheld recorder on, and putting it on the desk between us.

My immediate response to her actions was to close my mouth, because talking on tape was against the code of the streets. I wasn't in the street no more though, and if I was serious about staying out of prison, then I was gonna need this lady's help. It was now or never.

"I'm different because I survived. Most men, most young black men, don't get twenty-year sentences and make it out. Prison ain't designed for us to get out, it's designed for us to become permanent job security and 401K plans for people who run it. I'm different because I realized that in time to save my own life."

"Is that the only way you're different?" she asked.

"No. I'm different because in prison, you're only allowed to openly feel certain things, mainly anger. Not being allowed to feel for fear of judgement forces you to suppress all those other emotions that make people human. Then one day, you wake up and realize that you no longer know *how* to feel things like empathy or compassion. You realize you're different. Maybe something less than human," I admitted, reluctantly. My statement hung between us for a few seconds, but her eye contact never wavered and I didn't detect anything other than openness coming from her.

"Less than human, you say. Is that how you got the name 'The Lion'?" she asked, casually.

I shouldn't have been surprised she knew the nickname that had followed me into prison, especially since our sessions were court mandated, and came with access to my entire criminal file. I guess the surprise I was feeling came from how direct she was, because if she knew about "The Lion" then she knew I was nothing nice.

"That name was earned before prison. It was given in affection because of my first name and birth sign, but once I was inside, it took on a different meaning. Prison is a land of savages, just like the jungle, and I had to be at the top of the food chain. It was my destiny, I guess."

"That's an interesting statement, so why do you feel it was your destiny?" she asked, leaning back in her chair and crossing her arms over her chest.

"Because I always knew I was going to prison. I've lived my life a certain way, so finding myself behind bars was a guarantee."

"I want you to elaborate, so I think we should go back to the beginning," she suggested.

"The beginning? Oh, you wanna talk about my childhood and how good or bad it was."

"As cliché as it may sound to you, yeah, that's exactly what I wanna do because it'll help to put things into perspective for both of us," she said.

"If you say so. What do you wanna know?" I asked, sitting back and getting comfortable in my chair.

"Well, I don't want you to feel like we've gotta cover your whole life in this first one-hour session, because you don't. Let's try something easy, tell me about one of your earliest good memories."

On its face, her request did sound like an easy one, but she hadn't lived my life. Talking about spending more than half of my life in prison was hard enough, but now she was asking me to walk through a minefield in the dark.

"Take your time," she said encouragingly.

Part of me wanted to take her statement literally and stall until our session was complete, but there was a bigger part of me that wanted the help she could provide. Having done my homework on Dr. Davenport, I knew she was more than five-eight of well-built beauty. She was actually a respected psychologist. There may still be a stigma about mental health, but part of understanding that I'm different is understanding I need help to figure myself out.

"An early good memory, huh? I remember when I was about five years old and I was riding my little Bigfoot four by four through my neighborhood. There was this bird laying in the middle of the street and I could tell it was hurt, because it kept trying to fly with only one wing. To the average onlooker, it probably looked funny because the bird was just spinning in circles, but I wanted to help it so I drove into the street, got out and picked it up, put it in the back of my Bigfoot and drove it home to my mom. I ran in the house and pulled her outside so she could help the bird, but she didn't. She threw it in the woods and dragged me in the house, kicking and screaming."

"Why is this a good memory for you, Delontae?" she asked, confused.

"Because it taught me one of life's most valuable lessons, everybody dies and nobody cares."

ARYANNA

Chapter 3

"Sorry I missed your call. Is everything aight? Is Maleah good?" I asked, quickly.

"If you *really* cared about your daughter, you would've answered no matter what you were doing, nigga, or *who* you were doing. She's fine, but we need to talk," Jerika replied, with obvious attitude. As if my day wasn't long enough having to deal with a head doctor, I now had to endure the mind fucking only my baby mama could master. This was the same bitch who'd kept my daughter from me for my last few years inside, taken me to court for full custody, and now she was using the last few months before our child's eighteenth birthday to continue playing puppet master. It was times like this when I regretted ever sliding her the dick during our visits while I was locked up. Her saying that we needed to talk was the bell for the opening round of more bullshit.

"Okay, what's up?" I asked, pushing the rest of my Popeye's chicken aside, and sitting back in the restaurant's booth.

"When you gonna bring me some more money?"

"More money? Jerika, I just gave you five hundred dollars last week, what the fuck are you talking about?" I asked, annoyed.

"How far you think five hundred dollars go, nigga? That ain't nothing! Plus, don't act like you don't need to be playing catch up for all the years you missed."

"What does Maleah need, and why didn't she just call me?" I asked.

"I told her *I'd* call you, and whatever she needs I'll handle. You just bring the money," she replied, nastily.

Her attitude told me my daughter didn't need shit, but most likely my out of work, lazy, trifling-ass baby mama did.

"Look, whatever it is will have to wait until tomorrow because I'm not battling rush hour in D.C., and end up missing my curfew at the halfway house," I said.

"If you would've answered your motherfucking phone when I called, nigga, you could've made it out here before rush hour! You ain't shit and—"

I let her finish the rest of her sentence with the dial tone because I would be damned if she kept barking at me like shit. Instead of dealing with her bullshit, I hopped on Facebook and sent my daughter a message, asking her if she needed anything, and telling her to call me.

"Ayo, my man, you done here?"

I looked up from the phone to find a stocky-built nigga in a white t-shirt, standing next to my table, holding his girl's hand.

"Nah, bruh, I ain't done," I replied, resuming typing my message to Maleah.

"I'm saying, you ain't eating, you just playing on your phone. So why don't you let me and my lady get this booth?" he said.

Looking around the restaurant I noticed it was somewhat crowded, but there were other seats available. There just weren't any booths.

"Like I said, I'm not done, but I will be in a little while if you wanna wait," I replied, not bothering to look at him.

"Bae, please deal with this old nigga while I go to the bathroom, I'm trying to sit down and eat when I come back," his girl said, walking away.

I knew I had some gray hair in my dreads now, but I thought that made me look more distinguished, not old. And neither my face nor the solid body beneath my tailored Tom

Ford suit alluded to my thirty-nine years of age, so I didn't know what made this girl call me old. Hopefully, her dude was smarter than to be fooled by the gray hair.

"Listen, old head, we just trying to eat, not cause any problems. Understood?"

This time when he spoke, he put his hand on my shoulder. That was his mistake. After putting my phone in my pocket, I stood up to my full five-ten, which brought me eye-to-eye with my new friend. He opened his mouth to say something, but I wasn't interested in his words, as much as I was the opportunity he'd provided. Before he knew what happened, I drove my forehead into his mouth and nose, knocking out a tooth before he collapsed to the floor like he was attacking the linoleum. I could hear gasps coming from the people sitting close by, which prompted me to grab my tray and dump it while I strolled away casually.

"Ay, bruh!" someone called from behind me, I didn't turn around or stop, but I didn't quicken my pace either. In my mind, I knew what I'd just done could be considered assault, which was a direct violation of my probation, but running would only make me look more guilty. Besides, the crime in Washington, D.C. was too serious for the cops be worried about some punk ass assault.

"Ah, bruh...Lion!" the same voice called from behind me.

This time, I did stop on the sidewalk outside the restaurant and turn around. The short, brown-skinned dude walking towards me looked familiar, and him using my nickname showed a certain amount of familiarity, but that didn't mean he was a friend.

"I know you?" I asked, warily.

"It's Jay, ya young cousin, nigga!"

Having the name to go with the face helped to unlock the memory, and I let my guard down a little.

"What's up, fam, when did you get home?" he asked, pulling me into a half hug.

"About a month ago."

"Damn, why you ain't tell nobody? You know we would've thrown you a big-ass, welcome home party."

"I'm trying to stay under the radar, Cuz, you can understand that," I said, looking around for signs that someone had called the police over the unconscious man I'd left in Popeye's.

"Knocking niggas out in public ain't exactly staying under the radar, but I get what you're saying. Look, let me give you a ride somewhere, because it's probably best to put some distance between you and what just happened."

"Cool," I agreed, knowing public transportation might not get me out of the area fast enough. I followed my cousin to the parking lot around the side of the building, but I pulled up short when he hit the alarm to unlock a brand new burgundy LC 500 Lexus coupe. It may have been years since I'd seen or spoken to Jay, but I knew the signs of a dope boy.

"You clean?" I asked, seriously.

"Of course, I'm not trying to see you go back to the feds."

Something in me wanted to question him, but I gave him the benefit of doubt because we were family. And I climbed in the car.

"It's good to see you, Lion. It's been way too long, man. How's my auntie doing?" he asked, quickly putting Popeye's in the rear view mirror as he pulled off into traffic.

"She's fine, doing the same old shit. What about your mom?"

"Her health ain't too good, but the doctors are doing everything they can to keep her comfortable. I tried to get her to stay with me, but she wanted to go to hospice."

Part of me felt bad that my aunt Brenda had been fighting a losing battle against AIDS for the better part of twenty years, enduring that pain and suffering. Still, it would be a sad day when she was no longer here.

"How's the rest of the family?" I asked.

"You know them mufuckas is still crazy, but they fam, so we gotta accept them as they are. You got somewhere you need to be right now?"

"Nah, I got a few hours before curfew at the halfway house. Why?"

"Halfway house? Cuz, you ain't gotta stay at no damn halfway house. I got spots all over the city you can choose from," he offered.

"I appreciate that, Jay, but it's part of my probation that I gotta do ninety days in a halfway house. I gotta prove I'm legit."

"I hear that. Since you got some time though, you can ride with me to meet your little cousins because I gotta swing past me house real quick. Cool?" he asked.

"Ya, that's cool. How many kids you got now?"

"Shit, *too* many, my nigga. I got five, four boys and one girl, and they keep me *busy!*"

"Business must be good though," I replied, admiring the clean leather and new car smell of the coupe we were riding in. My comment earned me a chuckle as we glided to a stop at a red light.

"Yeah, business is good, but I'll never forget who taught me the business," he said, opening the glove box and tossing a wad of cash in my lap.

"We fam, you don't owe me shit, so—"

"I'm not giving you that because I owe you, Lion. I'm doing it because it's what you would've done if the roles were reversed. You've always been one of the realist niggas I've known, and I know I didn't hold you down properly while you were doing your bid, but I ain't never forgot you," he replied, pushing the money back towards me that I'd tried extending back to him. Despite the fact that we'd done a lot of dirt together growing up, and made moves in the streets, it still felt weird to take money from him now. I didn't feel like it was coming with expectations though, and that was a rare thing, even amongst family. I could front and act like I didn't need it. I mean, I was wearing Tom Ford from head to toe. The reality was that I'd spent every bit of the money I'd made doing construction work on this outfit, because I'd been determined to make a good first impression with the doctor. Not to mention, the five hundred dollars I'd given Jerika was gone already, and I had to come up with more in a hurry. Accepting this from my cousin would keep me out of the street for one more day.

"I appreciate it, my nigga. I got you when I'm seeing better days or when I get paid on my next construction job," I said, sliding the knot of bills into my pocket.

"It ain't nothing. I'ma help you get a better gig than that construction shit too."

"That's just a little temporary situation, you know, just to keep the peoples off my back and out of my business," I said defensively.

"I get it, but you better than that, fam. I got my hands in a few legit businesses, some strip clubs and a couple barber shops. I know you learned how to cut hair while you was in that mufucka."

"That's prison one-oh-one. Before we get into that though, I need to know that your other business doesn't cross paths with your legal business at any point," I said.

"Absolutely separate operations, not even connected for the purposes of washing money. My legit business interests are my retirement plan, because I'm not about to be in these streets forever. Nobody survives that long."

It was good to hear that my cousin understood that. We were separated in age by five years, but talking to him now made me feel like he was more on my level of maturity than when I left. We spent the rest of the thirty-minute drive catching up on old times, while he brought me up to speed on the city I loved so much. Once upon a time, I'd thought I'd owned these streets, thought I was bigger than any law governing them, and badder than any mufucka who wanted to take over. Twenty years for conspiracy to commit murder had changed my mind though, and helped me to understand the price of controlling the streets was too high. You had to pay in blood, and too much was never enough.

"Aight listen, I gotta run in here and pick up some money, but I'll be in and out," he promised, stopping in front of a run-down apartment building. Southeast D.C. had changed a lot, but the dope areas would never change.

"Jay, you can do that another time, bruh, I ain't trying to be-."

"Chill, Cuz, you ain't going in with me. Just sit tight, and if anyone comes up to the car, there's a nine millimeter Ruger under my seat," he said, hopping out of the car before I could get a word out.

Part of me wanted to hop out the car with him and beat his fucking brains loose, for having a gun in the car the whole time! I'd specifically asked if he was clean, and even if the gun was legal, that nigga *knew* I couldn't be around it because I was a convicted felon! Everything in me was screaming for me to get my ass out of this car and simply walk away, but I knew given my surroundings that could be a worse move. If I had my license, I would've slid behind the wheel and left his dumb ass, but I didn't and I wasn't about to risk getting pulled over.

"Just sit tight, he'll be back in a minute," I tried convincing myself out loud.

Five minutes later, I was cussing him out and calling him everything except the name his mom gave him, when the sudden sound of gunshots jerked my attention to the apartment building's entrance. Within seconds, the front door to the building opened and Jay stumbled out unsteadily on his feet. I had no idea what happened, but it was evident he was hurt and he needed my help. It wasn't exactly pitch black outside, but it was still dark enough that I had to grope around blindly under the driver's seat, until I felt the familiar coldness of steel against my fingertips. By the time I had the gun in my hand and the car door open, the shooter was right behind Jay, firing another round that put my cousin down on the sidewalk. Before I had time to analyze my actions, I was out of the car and the pistol was jumping to life in my hands, with a familiarity that turned my blood to ice. Two shots made the shooter's head disappear, but I didn't lower the gun as I ran to my cousin's side. Even in the evening's dusk, there was no denying Jay's soul was beyond this world. Leaving him wasn't right, but staying until the cops and coroner arrived wasn't an option. No explanation would get me out of handcuffs once the law was included, and no lawyer could keep me out of prison. I knew Jay would understand, but even if he wouldn't have, it didn't matter. He was dead, and I had to go.

Chapter 4

"Mr. Mathias," Dr. Davenport said, hesitantly.

"I know I don't have an appointment today, and you're technically not open yet, but I, uh, needed to talk to you," I said, rising from the spot by her office door I'd been sitting in since six a.m.

I knew she didn't open her doors to patients until nine o'clock, even though she arrived at eight, but last night's events had my mind going in so many directions that I needed a quiet voice. Death wasn't new to me, not even the death of someone I was related to, but the replications of my cousin's death had kept my eyes from closing once I finally made it back to my bed at the halfway house. I kept waiting for those flashing lights to interrupt the night and reclaim my soul, this time for good. When they hadn't come by sunrise, I decided to get on the move, and this had been the only destination that made sense.

"If you don't mind me eating breakfast while we talk, you can come in," she replied, unlocking the door to her reception area.

"Of course not. I'm really sorry for interrupting your morning routine."

"It's not a problem. I'm always here for my patients. Although, most of them do call first," she said, giving me a teasing smile over her shoulder.

"Point taken, I'll call first from now on," I replied, closing the door behind us and following her down the hall to her office.

Walking this same path yesterday, I'd felt apprehensive and uncertain, but I wasn't plagued by either of those feelings now. Dr. Davenport had a way of putting me at ease, but more than that, she had a way of making her environment feel safe. The times I'd experienced that in my life were few and far between.

"So, Delontae, tell me what happened," she said, sitting her purse and Dunkin' Donuts fast-food bag on her desk, before shimmying out of her jacket.

"What makes you think something happened?" I asked, quickly.

"Part of my job as a doctor is observation, so while your black slacks and white button-up are fresh and pressed, your eyes tell me that you haven't slept since I last saw you. The biggest indicator is that you showed up here, unannounced, and since everything in your life has taught you to keep secrets, the fact that you wanna talk means something happened."

Her analysis was logical, but nonetheless impressive, and it affirmed my decision to put faith in the good doctor.

"You're right, something did happen," I replied, taking a seat in the same chair I'd occupied yesterday.

"Go on," she prompted, taking her own seat and unpacking her breakfast sandwich.

"Uh, I'm not sure this is something you wanna talk about while you eat."

"That was part of the deal we just made outside. Don't worry, it takes more than conversation to disrupt my appetite, so tell me what's on your mind," she insisted.

"One of my cousins was murdered last night," I blurted out.

Despite her previous statement, my words froze her fingers over the sandwich's wrapper and her eyes immediately came up to meet mine.

"I-I'm sorry, Delontae. Do you know what happened?" She asked, leaning back in her chair, her breakfast clearly forgotten.

"He was shot, at least twice, in a bad neighborhood in Southeast."

"How do you feel?" she asked.

"How do I feel? What do you mean, how do I feel?"

"During our conversation yesterday, we talked about how you've had to suppress emotions for a big part of your life, but it's time we start to break that cycle. I want you to tell me how you feel about your cousin being murdered," she replied, encouragingly.

"I feel, I don't know. I guess I feel guilty."

"Guilty? Why guilty?"

"Because I didn't save him. His life was worth more than whatever the disagreement was that led to his death, and I didn't save him."

"Delontae, you couldn't have saved him because you weren't there when it happened. You *weren't* there, right?" she asked.

When I locked eyes with her, I saw she was looking at me differently, and I realized something in my expression was making her ask the wrong question.

"No, I wasn't there, but I feel partially responsible for the way he was living his life. He was five years younger than me, but we ran the streets together before I was locked up," I said.

At first, she didn't speak, she just silently evaluated me. I didn't know what she was thinking, but the longer the silence, the more wary I became.

"Would you mind closing the door, my receptionist should be in at any time and I don't want her to hear anything she shouldn't."

I immediately got up and complied with her request, even if I was thrown off by the suddenness of it.

"You know, I feel bad about interrupting your breakfast, so why don't I just schedule an appointment for later today or tomorrow?" I suggested.

"That's not necessary, plus I think there are some things we should clear up real quick. Please sit back down."

I reclaimed my seat, wondering where this conversation was about to go.

"I know your sessions with me are court mandated, but my practice is still a legitimate private practice. I only get court cases, because I do pro bono work. I say all that to say, I'm still a licensed doctor, who is bound by patient/doctor confidentiality, and I take that *very* serious. What you say to me, whether it's recorded or not, stays between us unless you confess to a murder, or you're planning a terrorist attack. You can trust me, Delontae, I promise you, I won't betray you."

Survival in the streets and prison depended largely on trusting your instincts. Before you could trust your instincts, you had to have them so you could spot bullshit several miles away. I relied heavily on my instincts and right now, I felt like this woman sitting across from me was being completely sincere with how she was coming at me. Plus, she'd laid out the qualifiers for which she'd have to divulge information about what we discussed.

"I understand what you're saying," I replied.

"Good, so let me ask you a question. Were you there when your cousin was murdered?" she asked, softly.

I'd had a feeling we'd be getting back around to this topic of discussion, but I still didn't know how much to tell her. Full disclosure was definitely off the table!

"Yeah, I was there. I saw his body drop and when I got to him I saw he was dead, but for obvious reasons I didn't stay."

"And?" she prompted.

"And? Everybody dies and nobody cares. I told you that."

"I don't think that's true for you anymore though, because it's obvious you care about what happened to your cousin."

"I care that I was somewhere I shouldn't have been, when something happened that'll attract the police's attention. I'm not going back to prison for my cousin's decisions, or for any other reason. I'd rather die than go back," I replied passionately. I could tell by the look on her face that she was taken aback by what I said, but I didn't see how lying would help either of us.

"They wouldn't really send you back to prison for witnessing a crime," she said, skeptically.

"Wouldn't they? I'm a convicted felon, which means I don't get the benefit of the 'wrong place, wrong time' excuse. I get the side eye, and the guilty 'til proven innocent judgment."

I could tell part of her wanted to argue, but she was intelligent enough to understand that I was speaking from a position of experience she couldn't relate to.

"So, is that why you wanted to talk to me, because you were in the wrong place at the wrong time? Or, because you felt guilt about the way your cousin was living his life?" she asked.

"Honestly, I don't know. From the moment I came home, I felt like I've been in limbo between my past and my future. I wanna move forward, but I have to keep looking over my shoulder to make sure my past doesn't pull me down, *and* I have to continuously check my peripheral vision for the cops. That's an immense amount of pressure, Doc."

"I agree. I think you're built to handle it though, because you have an awareness about you that few people in your position possess," she replied.

Maybe I was imagining it, but I thought I detected a hint of admiration in her tone.

"I guess I wanted to talk to you because I feel like no matter the topic or situation I'm encountering, you'll be able to understand or put it into perspective. I've never known anyone who could do that," I confessed.

"Is there no one else you talk to or confide in?"

"In this world, who can you really trust?" I asked, rhetorically.

"What about your girlfriend?"

Her question caught me off guard. Actually, it was the certainty with which she asked about a woman in my life, like she knew it to be a fact.

"I don't have a girlfriend," I replied, calmly.

My response earned me a look I couldn't quite decipher, but it made me defensive.

"Why are you looking at me like that? I *don't* have a girlfriend."

"So, who is the woman who's name appears on all of your paperwork?" she asked, smiling slightly.

Now I knew why she asked her question with so much certainty, but she was way off.

"That's not my girlfriend. She was my best friend, but it's complicated," I replied, vaguely.

"I get the feeling most of the people you have relationships with, fall into the realm of complicated. Companionship could help with the loneliness and isolation you feel, though."

"I never said I was lonely or isolated," I replied, defensively.

"You didn't have to, and you don't have to say it like it's a bad thing. You feeling lonely and isolated is a natural reaction to your environment change, because this world you're living in now is completely foreign to you. Believe it or not, there are people who haven't experienced what you have, but they feel lovely and isolated for different reasons. The advice I give them is the same I'll give to you. You have to *live* life and not simply exist. A woman might help that. Unless you're into something else."

"You got me fucked up," I said, before I could stop myself.

I thought my outburst would've put fear into her but instead, she smiled and fought to suppress her laughter.

"I didn't mean to offend you, but in this day and age, I have to leave the door open for my patients to express themselves without fear of judgment."

Her explanation checked my anger and allowed me to see things from her perspective. I actually felt kind of stupid for the way I'd come at her.

"I understand. For the record though, I never questioned your sexuality, not with the way you carry yourself."

"And what's that supposed to mean?" I asked, curiously.

"You move with confidence because you know you're attractive, and despite your incarceration, you're highly intelligent, which leads me to believe you understand the effect you have on women. Granted, your interaction with the opposite sex has been limited, but you're well versed in the art of observation, and you're *not* green. Oh, there's also the *several* solicitation of staff write-ups you got while inside," she said, smiling.

I didn't know *how* I kept forgetting she knew everything about me the authorities had on the inside.

"You know, you've got me at a severe disadvantage, because you know all about me, and I know *nothing* about you," I said.

"I find that hard to believe, Delontae, but in time you'll—"

A knock at the door interrupted our conversation.

"Come in," she said.

"I'm sorry to interrupt, but your first appointment is here, and she seems a bit distressed," the receptionist reported.

"Okay, Evelyn, thank you. I'll be out in a minute."

When the door closed, we simply stared at each other for a moment, and I wondered what exactly she was thinking.

"I'm not sure if I was any help to you this morning, and I really hate to push you out the door, but—"

"No, it's fine, and you did help me," I said, standing up to leave.

"Hold on," she said, picking up her pen and scribbling something down on a piece of paper. "Here, this is my personal number and I keep my phone on at all times."

"So, what happens if I call you in the middle of the night, won't your significant other feel some type of way?" I asked, accepting the slip of paper.

"Stop fishing, Delontae, just call if you need me"

"Whatever you say, Doc," I replied, laughing.

"I guess you can call me Su'ryah now."

38

Chapter 5

One week later

It had only been a couple days since I watched my cousin disappear into the ground, accompanied by fistfuls of dirt, but already the streets were buzzin' about who was next in line to take his spot. It had come to light that the nigga who killed Jay, the nigga I killed, was a hired hitta sent by a rival dealer looking to takeover Jay's territory. The only reason he hadn't stepped to the plate yet was because he didn't know who hit his hitta, and that had him looking both ways before he crossed the street. Lucky for him, I had no interest in the dope game. I paid my respects, and did my aunt Brenda a favor by splitting up his money between his baby mamas for the kids. He'd been smart to only tell his mom where he kept his nest egg, because all his baby mamas was gold digging, thirsty bitches. They each tried to get his Lexus coupe, but my aunt had gifted that to me, despite me not having a license yet. I had to park it a *long* way from the halfway house, because I damn sure didn't need them in my business. I'd learned a long time ago that everything was based on perception, and me driving a new Lex made it look like I was back in the streets. I was fighting against that backslide every day, which was why I had an interview today with a car dealership. I figured with being a burn hustler, who sold as many dreams as I had drugs, that selling cars would be a piece of cake.

"Mr. Mathis, he's ready for you," the secretary said, nodding towards the manager's office door. I stood and smoothed out any wrinkles I may have had in my new, navy blue Michael Kors suit, before making my way through the door.

"Good morning, Mr. Normal, thank you for seeing me," I said, extending my hand to the short, balding, middle-aged white man standing behind the desk.

"No problem, Mr. Mathis, have a seat. Before we get to your application and resume, I want you to tell me why you think you'd be a good fit for this industry."

"Well, naturally, I have a love for automobiles. I also believe that the secret to being a good salesman is being a people person, and that's something I was born with. I think that trait, and my willingness to learn, will make me an asset to this company," I replied, confidently.

"Okay, well let's take a look at your paperwork," he said, turning his attention to the computer on his desk.

My confidence slipped a little because I knew he would have questions about the holes in my resume, and the fact that I hadn't checked the box about felony convictions one way or another. It had been so long since my conviction that I technically wasn't obligated to check the box, but I was smart enough to know that lying would disqualify me in the eyes of potential employers. My only option was to gamble on my ability to finesse the situation and explain away any doubts this man had about me. For a long five minutes, Mr. Normal didn't speak or avert his eyes away from the computer's screen, and with each passing minute, I became less confident and more nervous.

"Well, your application looks to be in proper order, along with your resume. We'll keep both on file and contact you when and if we have something for you," he said, neutrally.

I knew his words were meant to give me hope at a position within this company, but I could see the bullshit clearly in his brown eyes. He wasn't taking my black ass any more serious than the others before him that had wasted my time with interviews since I'd been home. I was either over-qualified or they'd be in touch. The reality was that I was a black man who had the *nerve* to be a convicted felon, which meant my only opportunities came in the form of manual labor. Like my dark-skinned ancestors before me, I wasn't fit to work in the big house. I was nothing more than a field nigga.

"Thank you for your time," I replied, getting up and turning for the door, without bothering to shake the hand he offered.

I felt like if I touched him, I'd wanna touch him up with a few rights and lefts, and that would only lead to trouble. Instead, I made my way out of the building and to my car without causing a scene, and got the fuck away from there before I lost my temper.

I didn't have anywhere to be since it was raining, and the foreman I was working for had cancelled our job for the day. The thought crossed my mind to drop in on the doctor, but I wasn't trying to come off as too needy, or worse yet, too thirsty. Maybe I needed to take her advice and find a female to kick it with. I'd gotten plenty of "fan mail" while I was inside, and there were a few clicks trying to throw the pussy out of both pants legs in my direction. The only reason I hadn't tried to knock anybody down yet was because I'd been focused on doing everything I could to keep my P.O. off my ass. The time had come to make a move though. I pulled into a McDonald's drive-thru and ordered something to eat, and while I waited on my food, I decided to hop on Facebook. The first thing I noticed was a message from Jerika, telling me I wasn't shit, but I didn't bother opening it to read the rest of her rant. Instead, I went to my friends' list and scrolled them to see which name and picture caught my attention. I had to be real with myself about what I wanted though because complications were one thing I *wasn't* looking for. With that in mind, it made sense to go with someone familiar, which is why as soon as I saw Rahsheeda's face, I knew it was her I wanted. I quickly typed out an innocent enough message, asking how she was doing, and if we could get together to catch up sometime soon. I wasn't expecting her to see or respond to my message for a couple hours because she was probably at work, but to my surprise, my phone was alerting me to a notification right after I got my food out of the window. Her message was simple and to the point, she wanted me to come to her house now, and she'd given me the address. Putting the address into my GPS, I learned that she lived over an hour away in Virginia, but I knew she would make it worth my time. Without giving it a second thought, I was on the road headed to see my first love.

The story of how her and I came to be was the definition of complicated, but it was filled with more good times than bad. On some level I believed we'd always love each other, but that didn't mean we were meant to be together. I made the hour-and-fifteen-minute drive in forty-five minutes, finding her townhouse with no problem and feeling only a little nervous about reuniting with her. Right about now, I was regretting the onions on my quarter pounder with cheese, but there was nothing I could do about it.

By the time I got out of the car, she was standing in the doorway of her house, smiling and looking like she hadn't aged in the twenty years I'd been gone.

"I thought you would've at least got taller," I said, walking up to her.

"Fuck you, punk, I'm five foot and proud of it," she said, before taking a step and leaping into my arms. "I'm so glad you're home!" she squealed, hugging tightly.

"It's good to be home," I replied, walking with her in my arms up her front steps and into her house.

Once the door was closed, she immediately shoved her tongue in my mouth, giving me a much more thorough greeting. I'd anticipated having to kick a little shit at her to get her to give me the pussy, but her enthusiasm told me words were probably unnecessary. I had no idea where her bedroom was, but I spotted a couch in my peripheral vision and I made a clumsy beeline straight for it. When I sat down, she straddled me properly, reaching beneath the flowery spring dress she had on, and went straight for my zipper.

"When did you become-so-aggressive?" I asked, in between kisses.

"When I had to go so long without this," she replied, pulling my dick through the opening in my slacks and squeezing it.

I tried to prepare myself mentally for what was about to happen. But before I knew it, she'd raised up and plunged my dick inside her.

"Oh God, I'm glad you're home," she moaned, riding me in a slow circular motion that caused my eyes to roll out of focus. It felt like there was no air in the room, but I kept trying to breathe, and all I was taking in was the scent of our sex.

"Baby, baby D, I—"

"I know, I love you too," she whispered against my mouth, before kissing me hungrily.

That wasn't even *close* to being what I was about to say to her, but the pussy was too good for the truth right now. She was bouncing straight up and down on the dick while grabbing two handfuls of my dreads for leverage, and I was loving *everything* about her right now. I could feel myself wanting to cum, but I needed her to cum with me so I didn't embarrass myself. I grabbed her by her hips and forced her to go faster by pulling her down on top of me, while meeting her with upward thrusts. It sounded like a fist fight, but I could tell it was having the desired effect.

"Aw, Delontae, wait! Wait before you make me c-c-cum!" she pleaded, gripping my hair tighter. I ignored her words and listened to her body, continuing to feed her dick until the dam burst and our climaxes became a flood between us.

"Wel-come home," she panted, fighting to catch her breath. At the moment, I was beyond words, so I just held onto her with a shit-eating grin on my face. After going without it for so long, I'd forgotten how exceptional good pussy was. During my bid, I'd knocked down a nurse or two, but there was a difference between *regular* pussy and *good* pussy. Regular pussy could get on your nerves, but good pussy could change your life. With my dick still deep in the woman occupying my lap, I was lost in a haze of happy feelings, but not so much that I didn't hear the front door opening and closing behind me.

"Bitch, what the fuck!" a voice roared.

You would've thought the voice had Rahsheeda connected to a string, because it pulled her in its direction so fast, I barely felt my dick slide out of her.

"Keyon, baby, it's not what you think," she protested, immediately.

"I think you fucking some nigga in my *house!*" he yelled, slapping her hard enough to send her sliding across the floor.

By now I had my dick tucked away, intending to play it off with her even though I was pissed at her, but him putting his hands on her changed everything.

"You, you ain't gotta do all that, bruh," I said, sizing him up for weaknesses I could exploit.

He was easily six foot one or six foot two, weighing a solid two-hundred-fifty pounds, and even though he was my complexion, he was mad enough to be almost red in the face. Still, he wasn't nothing I hadn't dealt with before.

"Nigga, you in *my* house, fucking *my* bitch, and you got the nerve to be telling me what *I* should do!" he raged.

"Baby, I—"

He silenced her words with a swift kick to her stomach, and that's when shit went all bad for him. In two steps, I was on his blind side and I fired a right hook that instantly made his knees buckle, followed by a left hook that helped him locate the floor next to her. Before he could move, I hopped on him with the same swiftness as his girl had done me, and continued delivering blows that changed the position of his nose, along with the number of teeth he had.

"Delontae, stop!" Rahsheeda screamed.

I didn't pay her any attention, I just continued giving her man what we in the penitentiary referred to as '*the business*'.

"Delontae, *please!*" she pleaded, crying as she scooted closer to the melee. By now I could tell the man beneath me was barely conscious, but the sight of his blood was as intoxicating as her pussy had been moments ago.

"Delontae, Delontae! I'm gonna call the cops if you don't *stop!*" she yelled.

Hearing this froze my fist in mid-air, while I looked at her to see if she'd really said what I thought she did.

"What did you say?" I asked, softly.

"You heard me. Get off him or you're going to jail," she replied, flinging her body half across his to prevent me from swinging another punch.

Her actions had me completely dumbstruck and rendered me speechless for a full thirty seconds.

"Y-you wanna call police on me, for defending *you*?" I asked, shocked.

"You weren't defending me, you were *killing* him! You haven't changed, you're still the Lion, and you're still a *monster*! Just leave!" she demanded, crying over her boyfriend's ruined face.

I was at a loss for words. I mean I couldn't understand *what the fuck just happened*. Her reaction to how this shit had played out didn't seem real, but I knew it was. That meant I had two options right now, kill them both or get the fuck out of Dodge. Decisions, decisions.

Chapter 6

"Mr. Mathias, Dr. Davenport is expecting you, you can go right in," Evelyn said, waving me through the reception area. Sitting in the doctor's office was the last place I wanted or needed to be right now, but her text message reminding me that I'd already missed one court-mandated visit, made it impossible not to show it. Her timing was impeccable, considering I'd been on the way back from the disaster with Rahsheeda, trying to figure out which one of us was *really* crazy. I *still* couldn't believe what that bitch had threatened to do! Killing her and her bitch-ass nigga seemed entirely justified from my point of view, but unplanned murders were sloppy murders, and that raised the risks of getting caught. I'd had to let them live, but I made it clear that her and I were done for *good*.

"Well, I see you still remember how to get here," Su'ryah said, as soon as I walked into her office. I closed the door behind me and then walked over to her desk, sitting the paper bag I'd been carrying down in front of her.

"I brought you a peace offering to apologize. For not keeping our weekly appointment and for ruining your breakfast the last time I saw you," I said, taking a seat.

"I can't be bribed, Delontae, unless that's a steak and cheese sub from Danny's restaurant," she said, closing her eyes and inhaling mightily.

"With an apple pie and some fries," I replied, laughing at the look of guilty pleasure on her face.

"God, you're trying to make me fatter than I am already!"

"You're nowhere near fat, and you know it. Thick maybe, but definitely not fat," I insisted.

"That's a matter of opinion. All I know is that you're *killing* me right now, especially since I missed lunch today."

"Don't cheat yourself, treat yourself. And, I promise that we won't get into any heavy conversation until you're finished eating," I vowed.

"Honestly, it wouldn't matter because Danny's is my *weakness*," she said, finally giving into temptation and pulling food from the bag.

When it came to bringing her food, I'd had a tough decision to make, because two major food staples in D.C. were chicken wings with mumbo sauce, and steak and cheese subs. I'd gone with the latter, simply because I didn't see how a sane woman could resist an amazing steak and cheese.

"Oh wow, and you got the foot long? My hips can't stand that type of action," she protested.

As soon as she said it, I could tell she realized the sexual response she left herself open for, but I didn't say anything. I did smile though.

"You gotta help me with this, and before you open your mouth to argue, you need to understand that refusing is not an option," she said, pushing half of the sub in my direction.

After grabbing a few napkins from the bag, I picked up the sub and took a bite. She hesitated for a moment, watching me closely, but soon followed my lead and attacked her half.

"So, why haven't I heard from you?" she asked around a mouthful of food.

"Just been busy. My cousin's funeral was a few days ago, so I had some family business to deal with."

"Your cousin's funeral, Jaylon was his name, right?" she asked.

Her question caused me to stop chewing and look at her closely, because I knew I'd never mentioned him by his full government name. I was also sure there was nothing in my file about Jay.

"I can tell by the look on your face that you're trying to figure out how I know his name, so I'll save you the trouble and enlighten you. His name was mentioned on the nightly news, which I happened to catch the same day I last saw you. The news also mentioned how the man who shot your cousin was found laying only a few feet from him, with two bullets in his own head. I found that interesting," she said, taking another bite of her sandwich, and chewing thoughtfully.

I followed her lead so she wouldn't see how nervous I was right now, taking another bite of the sub and chewing slowly.

"Why do you find that interesting?" I asked.

"I think you know why I found that interesting, Delontae, please don't insult my intelligence."

"Okay, so what is it you're trying to say to me?" I asked, tired of playing games.

"I'm not asking you anything, because I'm sure if I *were* asking you anything about that night, I wouldn't want to know the answer. Maybe you know who killed the man who killed your cousin, maybe you don't. What *I* know is that everything in the dark comes to light eventually."

"Indeed it does," I replied calmly.

"I do have other questions I'd like to ask you though."

"More stuff about my childhood?" I asked, sarcastically.

"Perhaps, but let's start with what happened to your hands."

Looking down, I noticed that my hands had started swelling, and there were still droplets of blood covering my knuckles. A careless mistake by me, and now it was a costly one.

"Do you want the long story or the short one?" I asked, sitting the rest of my sandwich back on her desk.

"Whichever you want to tell."

I thought about how best to go about what I wanted to say, because I didn't want to say too much, even though her letting the subject of my cousin's death go inspired trust.

"I took your advice about, uh, trying to connect with a woman. It's been awhile, so I figured going with a known quantity was my best move, and I reached out to a woman I had history with."

"What kind of history? What I mean is, did you two end on good enough terms that you could double back for a booty call?" she asked, seriously.

"We have *a lot* of history, some good and some bad, but it never ended bad. I got locked up, and life doesn't stop for the outside world, so she moved on. We were each other's first loves. I mean, she was the first girl I got pregnant."

"So, you have a child with this woman? I thought you only—"

"No, we don't have a kid. Her mom made her have an abortion because she was only twelve years old, and I was only thirteen, but the whole experience bonded us in a way. It may sound weird, but it made us love each other more. For years I hated her mom, and I honestly wanted to kill her for killing my kid, but later I understood she did it to protect her family."

"Protect her family? From whom?" she asked, sitting her sub down and picking up her steak fries.

"That's complicated, but I'll try to explain. I met Rahsheeda, that's her name, because my uncle was talking to her mom. At that time, her mom was doing a bid, but when she got out she hooked up with my uncle. Rahsheeda and I didn't know they'd end up getting married when we started fucking, and by the time they did marry, shit had already gone too far between us. We didn't care what anybody thought, and our family didn't care because they made sure we saw each other as much as possible. Probably because all my uncle was really worried about was smoking crack with my mom, so our relationship was the perfect cover and the lesser of two evils. The problem was that my uncle and Rahsheeda were close, and when she turned up pregnant, her mom didn't know if the baby was mine or her husband's. She couldn't take the risk."

I could tell by the way her mouth was hanging open that my revelations had just blown her mind, but she recovered quickly.

"Do you think it was your uncle's baby?" she asked, calmly.

"I stopped asking that question years ago. For it to be true, that would mean that my uncle was a pedophile, and that's not something I can believe. I was abused when I was younger, but my uncle never gave me that uncomfortable feeling."

"Y-you were abused. How so?" she asked, startled by the revelation.

"You mean *that's* not in my file? I was abused sexually, twice. I don't remember much about the first time it happened, because I was only about five or six, I just know there was a man with me under the covers. The second time it happened, I was eight and the female babysitter was twelve or fourteen. She locked us in a room and things happened," I replied, vaguely.

"Did you tell anyone when these incidents happened?"

"Doc, I grew up in the crack era, and most of my family was criminals and fiends. I used to walk the streets after midnight at five years old. I got caught trying to sell crack at recess in the first grade. I was no one's priority, so who was I gonna tell? How was I supposed to know it was wrong? I wasn't taught stranger danger, I thought that you gotta hustle to survive, because ain't nobody giving you *shit* in this world. They only want to take from you," I replied, emotionlessly.

For a moment she simply stared at me, but I knew she wasn't seeing the man sitting in front of her. She was envisioning the little boy who had to steal food so he wouldn't go hungry, or maybe she was even seeing the kid who literally learned how to pull heists at his mother's side. Whatever she was seeing, it was all true. It was all a part of my story, but it was just chapters in the book, because I would decide how I wanted it to end.

"Did you ever confront your uncle about his relationship with Rahsheeda?" she asked, trying to mask the fact that she was visibly shaken.

"What would've been the point? That's a lie he would've died with, and if he had admitted something like that, I would've killed him without hesitation."

"You loved her that much?"

"I thought I did, but what happened today has forever changed my opinion," I replied, becoming angry all over again just thinking about the bullshit she had me involved in.

I quickly ran down the events of my day to the good doctor, embarrassed by my behavior now that I was looking back on it. I probably could've handled the situation better, or at least not tried to turn ole boy's face into hamburger meat, but hindsight was twenty-twenty.

"Wow. Has it been like this for you your whole life?" she asked.

"What do you mean?"

"I mean, I don't think you go looking for trouble, but it damn sure has a GPS on your ass," she replied, without humor.

"You're the first person I've ever had acknowledge that. Most people just assume that I'm on complete bullshit all the time, and therefore I deserve what I get."

"Well, I don't think that. I believe you've made some bad decisions in your life, but it sounds like life has put you in some fucked-up situations too. Knowing that you can't be involved in *anything* or you risk going back to prison, I really don't see you putting yourself in the middle of whatever happened to your cousin. And, this shit that happened today is just *crazy*! All you were trying to do was get your dick wet, and that turned into a shit show," she said, shaking her head.

Her candor threw me off for a second, but we were both adults, and I had no doubt that she knew what good dick felt like.

"My life is a mess, Doc, I guess that means I'm beyond saving," I said, half-jokingly.

"Actually, the fact that you don't use your past as a crutch or as justification for bad deeds, leads me to believe you want to change. I think deep down, you understand that a lot of things in life led you to the water, but it was you who chose to drink it. Owning bad behavior is a character building trait, so I think there's hope for you."

"You're probably the only one, but it's still good to have a fan," I replied, smiling and picking up the rest of my sub.

"You keep bringing me this good food and I'ma be a *big* fan!" she said, grabbing her own sub since she was done with the fries.

"You women are always complaining about your weight. Be real with yourself, because we both know that don't no man wanna fuck a stick figure. We want something to hold on to, someone we can take to Mama's house for Sunday dinner and know we won't get embarrassed by your bird eating. You know *damn well* you can't bird eat at no black woman's house, especially when she been slaving over that good food in that hot ass kitchen!" I said, laughing.

"You ain't lying about that, but I ain't had a home-cooked meal in a long time. Not since my parents passed away."

Hearing this wiped the smile right off my face and made me feel bad, even though there was no way for me to have known.

"I'm sorry to hear that. How long has it been?" I asked.

"Just over five years, but some wounds don't heal with time."

"True. I have an idea, why don't you let me take you out for some good home cooking?" I suggested.

"I can't do that, Delontae, you're my patient and—"

"And blah, blah, blah. Listen, we ain't selling secrets to the Chinese or trying to help Isis take over America. We're just two people that happen to like home-cooked food, and I know the *best* cook in the entire District of Columbia," I said, reasonably.

"How you gonna say that and you ain't had my cooking?" she asked, looking offended.

"We'll get to that later. For now, dinner is on me. What do you say?"

The hesitation was clear in those sparkling blue eyes, but I still saw part of her wanted to give in.

"I'll think about it," she said, slowly.

I was just about to put the pressure on her when my phone started going off. I would've ignored it, but it was Maleah's ring tone, and I would *never* ignore her.

"I need to take this," I said, pulling out my phone and standing up.

"Hey Maleah, what's up, sweetheart?"

"Daddy? Daddy, I'm in trouble. I need your help."

ARYANNA

Chapter 7

"Doc, I really appreciate this, and I promise I'll pay you back as soon as I can," I reassured her.

"It's okay, Delontae. I told you before the ride over here that I wouldn't have offered to help if it was a problem for me. Besides, now I get to meet your daughter," Su'ryah, replied, smiling.

"I just wish it was under better circumstances," I said, looking around the dingy Third District police station.

I'd seen my fair share of cop hangouts, but this was the first time I was on the other side of the glass posting bail for someone else. It absolutely broke my heart that it was my flesh and blood, my only child, being held back there in the filth of a jail cell. I never wanted that for her and sadly, I knew it would forever change her.

"I can't believe she got caught stealing," I said, shaking my head.

"Believe it or not, it happens more often than you think. In most cases it's a cry for help, so don't judge her, just try to understand her."

"Su'ryah, I'm the *last* person to cast the first stone, trust me. And, when I say I can't believe she got caught stealing, I'm saying that because her mom, aunt, and grandma are some of the best thieves on the East Coast. I know she learned this shit at their feet."

"Wow. You don't encourage Maleah to do stuff like this though, right?" she asked.

"I'd never want my daughter to experience the things I have, especially not when it comes to being caught up in the system. I'm simply acknowledging how she was raised and taught how to survive, I'm not condoning it."

"That's good. I'm interested to know how you're gonna handle this situation with your daughter *and* her mother," she said.

"One step at a time. There she is," I said, watching Maleah be escorted through the last set of doors with bulletproof glass. She looked so much like me, that I thought I was reliving my youth.

"Hi Dad," she said softly, giving me a hug and burying her head in my stomach.

"Hi, sweetheart. You okay?"

"I'm fine. Can we get out of here please?" she asked.

"Yeah, let's go," I replied, taking her hand and leading her out of the police station to the parking lot.

"Whose car is this? And who are you?" Maleah asked, finally noticing Su'Ryah.

"My name is Su'Ryah, I'm a friend of your dad's."

"The car is mine, it was a gift. Su'Ryah was nice enough to put up the money for your bond so I didn't have to leave you in there longer, or call your mom," I said.

"Thank you for helping my dad get me out," Maleah said, avoiding Su'Ryah's grace.

"It's not a problem, really. You two probably have a lot to talk about, so I'm gonna go. Delontae, I'll see you soon, right?"

"Definitely, and thanks again for your help," I replied, sincerely. I watched to make sure that she got behind the wheel of her 2018 silver Cadillac CT6 and pulled off, before turning back to my daughter.

"You wanna get something to eat?" I asked.

"Sure."

After opening the passenger door and putting her into the car, I got behind the wheel and put the police station in my rear view.

"Where do you wanna go eat?" I asked.

"Are you mad at me?" she countered.

"I don't know about mad. Disappointed, yes, but to be mad makes me feel like I'm passing judgment on your mistakes, and we both know that I'm not qualified to do that. I do wanna know what happened though."

"I was sloppy. I was in Nordstrom's looking at watches and I made the mistake of not looking for *watchers*. A plainclothes cop spotted me and took me in," she replied, dejectedly.

"Why were you stealing, Maleah?"

"To make money," she said, simply.

"You don't have to do that, though. I told you to tell me if you need something."

"Dad, you *just* came home from prison and I'm supposed to believe you've got money to support me *and* you?" she asked, skeptically.

"You're supposed to believe that the last thing I want is for you to make decisions in the moment that'll fuck up your future. Therefore if you need something, *anything*, you come to me and we'll work it out together. Okay?"

"That *sounds* good, but any money you give my mom will never make it to my hands, so—"

"You're almost an adult, or didn't you just figure that out in the bullpen with them grown-ass woman? There ain't no need for your mom to be playing middle man between me and you, so if you need something, no matter how big or small, I want you to come to me. Understand?" I asked, looking over at her.

"If you insist."

"I do. Now, let's figure out what to tell your mother," I said, not looking forward to that particular conversation at *all*.

59

"There's really nothing to tell. If she'd been a better lookout, then—"

"Whoa, whoa, whoa! Hold the fuck up, your mom was *there*? She was in the motherfucking store *with* you?" I asked in complete disbelief.

"Yeah, she was there."

I didn't know what to say. My brain was so consumed with increasing rage that I was rendered speechless! Despite having received three hot meals and a guaranteed place to lay my head for most of my life, I still understood the struggle out here in the streets was real. That *still* didn't justify Jerika doing dirt in the streets with our daughter! That was beyond reckless, it was bad parenting, plain and simple and I understood it all too well, because I'd walked the same path with my own mom. I'd be damned if my child followed in my footsteps.

"How long has this been going on?" I asked, fighting for calm, so Maleah wouldn't mistake my anger as being directed at her.

"I don't know, since I was about ten years old, I guess."

"Why didn't you tell me, sweetheart?" I asked, saddened by my daughter's stolen innocence, and my inability to protect her from that happening.

"You know why I didn't tell you, Dad. Aside from the fact that I didn't want you and mom fighting, and me getting my ass whooped for telling you what was going on, I also knew there was nothing you could do from where you were."

It hurt even more to know that what she said was absolutely true. I couldn't have done anything except made it worse for her. I was home now, though.

"I can't change your past any more than I can change my own, but I can damn sure contribute to your future and make it better," I vowed.

"Dad, you don't even know what I want for my future."

"You're right, I don't, so why don't you tell me," I said, pulling up in front of Lucy's Takeout.

"Believe it or not, I wanna go to college after I graduate high school, somewhere far away from everybody. I don't have the grades for an academic scholarship, and I definitely don't have the money to pay for my own tuition, so I guess it's a pipe dream."

"Not a pipe dream, sweetheart, just a dream and there's nothing wrong with dreaming. Don't *ever* stop dreaming," I said, emphatically.

"Dreams are for suckers, at least that's what my mom says."

"I don't give a fuck what your mom says, because this is *your* life, not hers. You gotta start living for you, and chase those dreams. You gotta believe in yourself, even when no one else does because if you don't, then the world you're about to step into will swallow you whole. You don't want that to happen, do you?"

"No," she replied, quickly.

"Good, 'cause I got an idea. Let's talk about it over some wings and mumbo sauce."

"Your treat," she said, smiling for the first time, before opening the door and getting out.

I followed her into the restaurant and we ordered our food, finding a booth by the window to sit in.

"So, here's the plan. You're gonna finish out your last few months of high school, and you're gonna apply to all colleges you want to attend. That car sitting out front is gonna guarantee that your first two years of school are paid for, and I'm gonna work my ass off to cover your last two years."

"Dad, you can't sell your car—"

"I can and I will. Besides, I don't even have a license. Your future is more important than any car or other material possession, so don't argue because I'm selling it. All I want you to worry about is keeping your grades up and finding a good school."

"Okay. I'll probably go stay at my cousin Whitney's house for a while anyway, because I really don't think I could be around her and not wanna say something crazy," she said, shaking her head angrily.

"Just avoid her, but I expect to hear from you daily because if your little ass disappears, I'm out five hundred dollars."

"No disappearing acts, Dad, I promise," she replied, sincerely.

A waitress brought us our food and our conversation switched to less stressful topics while we ate. There was so much I missed in Maleah's life, and even more that I had to learn about her as a person, so I treasured the moments we got to spend together. Before I knew it, almost two hours had passed and darkness was preparing to take over the city. I didn't want our bonding time to end, but I had one important stop to make before my curfew.

"Come on, I'll take you to your cousin's house," I said, standing up and leaving a tip before we left.

Luckily, we didn't have far to travel because I was determined to make my next stop, and I didn't know how long it would take.

"I expect to hear from you sometime tomorrow, and you better stay your ass out of trouble," I said, passing her a fifty-dollar-bill once I'd brought the car to a stop in front of her cousin's building.

For a second, she just looked at me before taking the money from my hands.

"Dad, can I ask you a question?"

"Of course, sweetheart, what's up?"

"You're not hustling, right? I mean, I appreciate everything you've been doing for me since you've been home, but I don't want to lose you again for any reason," she said, worry written all over her face.

"No baby, I'm not hustling, I promise."

The way she looked at me made me feel like she was trying to get a good look at my soul, but I was okay with that, because I was hiding nothing.

"I love you, Dad," she said, giving me a hug and a kiss.

"I love you too."

I made sure to watch her go into the building and make it to the apartment on the third floor. Once she was inside, I pulled off, embracing all the rage and fury I'd been suppressing for hours. I could taste the hate on my tongue, which made me understand my current destination probably wasn't a good place for me to go, but that didn't stop me.

Twenty minutes later, I crept into a familiar neighborhood on foot, knowing that to drive my Lexus into the projects, could create a memory for someone that would come back to haunt me. Thankfully, I didn't encounter anyone I knew, and the building I needed to go in didn't have a bunch of people loitering around it. I made my move quick, walking without hesitation in my steps and going straight for the last apartment on the first floor. My first round of knocks went unanswered, but when I started banging like the police, I heard the deadbolts start to turn.

"Nigga, what the fuck is wrong with you? Why you beating on the door like that?"

"It's good to see you too, Jerika, can I come in?" I asked, pushing past her before she had the chance to respond.

"What do you want, Delontae? Maleah ain't here."

"I can wait for her, are you expecting her home soon?" I asked, walking through the living room and dining room.

"No, she spending the night at a friend's house, so you can come back some other time. Better yet, call and she'll meet you somewhere, because I don't want you here. Why the fuck are you roaming through my house?" she asked, angrily.

I ignored her and kept going from room to room, feeling my fury grow stronger because of the lies coming from her mouth. It was time to put an end to the bullshit.

"She's at a friend's house, huh?" I asked, coming to a stop in the hallway where Jerika was standing with her hands on her hips.

"Yeah, she—"

The next lie was frozen in her throat as my hands vice-gripped around her neck.

"You nothing-ass bitch. You taught my daughter to steal and then you had the *nerve* to let her get caught," I growled, through clenched teeth, squeezing tighter.

She looked like a fish out of water, but her eyes still shone brightly with anger and defiance. I wanted them to shine brightly with fear.

"You don't *deserve* to be a mother, bitch, and I wish I'd never gotten you pregnant," I whispered, pulling her right up to my face so she could see the absolute loathing in my eyes.

The sound of her wheezing for breath was music to my ears and I listened to it closely like I would my favorite song. It took me a second to realize when it stopped. The realization of what that meant came quicker.

Chapter 8

When I finally took my hands away from Jerika's neck, her lifeless body collapsed to the floor at my feet. The sound of her body hitting the hard wood sounded an awful lot like the judge banging his gavel, and sending my black ass back into the depths of hell. Anyone else in my position might've been trying to rationalize or justify a crime of passion defense, so they could do the right thing and call for help. I was smart enough to understand that shit only worked for white people on TV, so I did the right thing for myself, and started looking for all the fire accelerants I could find. Luckily, Jerika kept plenty of liquor in the house, and I ran from room to room emptying every bottle I could, saving only one to douse her with. After that, I went through and took all the batteries out of her smoke detectors and turned the gas stove on, before I went back to her bedroom to light the blaze. In the back of my mind, I had aligning thoughts of guilt about who else might get hurt by me burning down an entire apartment building, but I pushed that away and used Jerika's lighter to start the party. The fire caught immediately, forcing me to make a quick exit from the apartment while trying to remain unnoticed or easily forgettable. I made it to the front desk without running into anybody, but instead of pushing through it and merging with the night, I paused. Self-preservation dictated that I keep going, but the thought of somebody's kid sleeping peacefully somewhere in this building, made me pull the fire alarm. I convinced myself that was the best I could do as I stepped into the darkness, and put my latest indiscretion behind me. I didn't stop hearing the sound of prison doors slamming until I slid behind the wheel of my car and pulled off in the opposite direction of the growing commotion. My first impulse was to go back and pick up Maleah because she would need comforting, but right now I needed an alibi. Pulling out my phone, I scrolled through my contacts until I found the number I was looking for, and then I called it.

"Hey, I'm sorry to bother you, but um, I—"

"I figured you might call, and it's okay. Are you still with your daughter?" Su'Ryah asked.

"No, I took her to stay with her cousin for the night. We talked, and it was mostly good."

"But, there was obviously some bad too, so why don't you come see me and we can talk about it?" she suggested.

"You want me to come to your house?" I asked, surprised.

"No, I'm back at the office. I had some paperwork to finish up. You can come here, I'll leave the door unlocked for you."

"Okay, I'll be there in about fifteen minutes," I replied, hanging up. Part of me knew it was fucked up to use someone who was just trying to help me, but to my way of thinking, I didn't have a choice. I couldn't give up my freedom again. I cruised through the city with my eyes wide open for cops, and thankfully I made it to the doctor's office without spotting a single one. True to her word, Su'Ryah left the outer office door unlocked and I made my way down the darkened hallway to her office.

"You work too hard," I said, creeping into the room and startling her.

"Boy, you almost gave me a heart attack! You can't walk any louder?" she asked, fighting to calm her nerves.

"I apologize, old habits die hard. I'm surprised you don't have any type of protection, especially being a beautiful woman, alone in this big, bad city."

Her response was to pull the baby nine millimeter pistol from her lap and smile at me.

"Still fishing for information about me, huh? Well, I'm from this big, bad city, so I know how to handle myself," she replied, convincingly.

"Whatever you say, sweetheart," I said, putting my hands straight up in the air while walking towards her. This made her laugh, and the sound of it was effortless sexiness.

"You really are crazy, huh?" she asked.

"I told you from the beginning that you would have to be the judge of that," I replied, taking my usual seat.

Even though she still had on her royal blue pantsuit that gave her an all-business appearance, I could tell she was more relaxed and capable of kickin' it like a real person.

"So, am I interrupting some important work?"

"Actually, you are, but it's okay because now you can help," she replied, opening her lower desk drawer and pulling out a bottle of Patrón with two clear plastic cups.

"Oh, wow. Doc, are you trying to get me drunk?"

"Well, you know the saying, a drunk man tells no tales," she replied, smiling while she poured us both a healthy shot.

"Besides, after bailing your daughter out of jail, I'd say it's a safe bet that you could use a drink. You wanna tell me about your conversation?"

Her question brought back immediate memories of me choking the life out of my baby mama. It forced me to down the shot she'd given me and push my cup towards her for another.

"Well, the good thing I learned is that Maleah doesn't wanna be 'bout that life, she wants to go to college and further her education. She thought that was a pipe dream because she doesn't have the grades for a scholarship, and money is *more* than tight, but I managed to assure her that I'll pay for college."

"You will?" Su'Ryah asked, raising an eyebrow as she poured me another drink.

"Calm down, I'll be selling my car to pay for the first couple years, and I'll do honest work to cover the rest."

"Hmmm. That's admirable, Delontae, truly."

"You sound surprised," I replied, slightly offended.

"Oh, I'm always surprised when it comes to you. It wasn't long into our first session that I realized you're not what you appear to be in black and white, but that's a great thing. So many men in your position are bitter, or filled with so much hopelessness for their future, it's like talking to a man who's dead, but too stubborn to admit it. You didn't let them kill your spirit while you were inside, I can tell that just by looking in your eyes. It's…"

"It's what?" I prompted when she didn't finish her sentence.

"Nothing, I was gonna say the wrong thing. Tell me about the rest of your talk with Maleah."

"Oh nah, now you *gotta* finish that sentence!" I insisted, smiling.

For a minute she just stared at me, sipping her drink, but the look I gave her made it clear I wasn't letting this topic of conversation go.

"I guess you *are* stubborn. Fine, I was gonna say that it's sexy that you didn't let them break you. The world needs more black men," she said, blushing slightly.

I hid my smile behind my own drink, allowing her words to hang between us for a moment. Part of me wanted to pounce on what I perceived as an opportunity, but Su'Ryah was the type of woman you took your time with. She was too smart to play checkers, so any move I made had to be with a chess master's calculation and patience.

"Thank you for that compliment, it means a lot coming from you. As for my conversation with Maleah, she told me her mother had actually been with her in the store. Not only that, she's been boosting with her mom since she was ten years old."

"Wow. I know you suspected as much, but how did it make you feel to hear your daughter confirm it?"

I knew I had to choose my words carefully, because this conversation could come back to bite me in my ass, sooner than later.

"I mean, it hurt me of course, because my baby never got the chance to *be* a baby. Growing up that fast and being introduced to those elements of life can have lasting effects on someone, so I'm thankful that Maleah is still focused on her education," I replied.

"That's definitely a blessing. What about your anger though?"

"What anger?" I asked, polishing off my second drink under her intense scrutiny.

"So, we're gonna play games now, Delontae? I thought you had more respect for me than that."

"You're right. Of course I'm angry, but I couldn't let my daughter see that, or she might've felt like it was directed at her," I said, telling a half-truth.

"That was very intuitive of you, and I take it that part of your conversation went well. Which means you're here to discuss your anger with me," she reasoned.

"I guess so. I'd much rather table that conversation for our next session though, and talk about you instead."

"I'm not *that* drunk yet, but what would you like to know if I were?" she asked, pouring us both another shot.

"Let's start with where you're from in the city?" I asked.

"Born and raised in the slums of Barry Farms."

It was my turn to be surprised by a revelation, because the neighborhood she came from was full of nothing but dope boys and misfits.

"If you don't mind me asking, how the *fuck* did you make it out of that neighborhood to become who you are now?" I asked, impressed.

"I didn't let it break my spirit."

"Damn, that's sexy," I whispered, looking at her through different eyes.

"Thank you, but I can't take all the credit. I had good parents and a good grandma to protect me, and guide me in the right direction."

"How come you don't have a good *man*?" I asked, impulsively.

"Damn, you trying to get all in my business, ain't you?"

"I'm sorry, I didn't mean—"

"Calm down, I'm fucking with you. Men tend to complicate things, and I don't really have time for complications in my life," she confessed.

"You don't get lonely?"

"Maybe, maybe not. Being alone is not the same thing as being lonely, so I guess the answer to your question is no," she replied, tossing her shot back.

I was sure her words probably sounded true to her ears, because that's the lie she was used to telling herself, but I saw something different in her eyes.

"You're a beautiful woman, why deny yourself the pleasures that come with that?" I asked.

"Who said I deny myself pleasure?" she countered, smiling mischievously.

"Touché, but you don't strike me as the type to give the pussy away."

"You're right, it's *way* too good for that," she replied, laughing.

"Oh yeah, you're *definitely* drunk."

"You think so, huh? Well, even if that's the case, you know I'm not lying to you," she said, looking me directly in the eyes. The dog in me was ready to say some slick shit, but the gentlemen in me kept it cool.

"Come on, Doc, you've done enough work for tonight. Let's get you in an Uber so you can go home," I suggested, finishing my shot and standing up.

"I'm *not* drunk, Delontae, so I don't need to take an Uber. I will agree to call it a night though, if you'll hang around for a minute and walk me out."

"Just don't point your gun at me again," I replied, smiling.

Her response was to toss the pistol in my direction, which I instinctively caught and tucked into the waist of my pants. I didn't question how big of a mistake I was making. I just went with the moment. She quickly organized her paperwork and hid the bottle of Patrón back in her desk drawer before standing up, grabbing her purse, and putting her suit jacket on.

"I'll take Lucille back now," she said, coming around her desk and stopping in front of me with her hand out.

"Uh, Lucille?"

"Yes, Lucille, doesn't everybody name their pistol?" she asked, laughing.

"Surrre, I named all my guns," I replied, sarcastically, giving her the pistol back.

Once she took it and put it away, I thought she would make a move for the door but instead, she simply stood there in front of me with a curious look on her face. I'd been nothing but a gentleman anytime I was in her presence, but she was a beautiful woman, and being this close to her was becoming quickly intoxicating.

"You sure you're not drunk?" I asked, seriously.

"Positive, why?"

My response was to gently take her face in my hands and kiss her soft lips with barely restrained hunger. Her mouth tasted like Patrón and strawberries, and as our tongues danced to a slow and sensual rhythm, I became drunk on the taste of reciprocated lust.

"You're a good kisser," she whispered, pulling back a little to look up into my eyes.

"I'm a better lover," I replied, reclaiming her mouth with my own, while tossing her purse in a chair and backing her slowly into her desk.

We worked in unison, pushing the paperwork on her desk aside, while getting her suit jacket off and her pants unbuttoned, so I could push them down over her ample hips. By the light of the moon, she was a vision of beauty, wearing only a sleeveless white blouse with matching white crotchless boy shorts.

"Nice panties," I commented, smiling.

"Glad you approve," she replied, quickly returning the favor of helping me undress until I was only wearing my pants and underwear around my ankles.

"Nice dick," she commented.

"Glad you approve," I replied, lifting her up on the desk and stepping in between her spread legs.

I reclaimed her succulent lips while simultaneously pushing my way inside her tight pussy as fast as I dared, immediately falling in love with how well we fit together. "Go, go slow," she whispered into my mouth, wrapping her legs around my waist and pulling me closer. The feeling of us throbbing in sync told me that it was in my best interest to do as instructed, so I did. My strokes into the depths of her were slow, but thorough in the exploration of her pleasure principles. Right before I reached the bottom of her well, she would squeeze me so tight that I had to remind myself to breath as I pulled back, and dove inside her again. We spent countless minutes playing the game of give and take, pushing each other to new heights with increasing speed, until the world shattered around us. We climaxed together, clinging onto each other in a breathless death grip that conveyed our satisfaction without words. I could feel her heart pounding inside her chest just like mine, and I knew with absolute certainty I'd found a woman who had changed my life forever. We stayed locked together until the sweat on our skin cooled and our heart rates slowed, and even then I only moved to bring our mouths together for more communication without words. With a kiss, I told her how much I enjoyed what had just transpired and hopefully, how much I appreciated the gift she'd given me. To my delight, her kiss was as enthusiastic as everyone before it had been.

"You lied to me," I accused, with mock irritation.

"About what?"

"You said your pussy was good, when you should've used another adjective like *great, dangerous,* or even *addictive*, but definitely not just good," I replied, smiling.

"Addictive, huh? Does that explain why your dick is still inside me?"

"Do you want me to take it out?" I asked, leaning in to kiss my way up her neck slowly.

"I have to admit, it's been awhile since I've been in this, or any sexual position, so I don't mind you staying a little longer. I wouldn't mind taking this somewhere more comfortable than my desk, though."

To my ears, it sounded like she was inviting me back to her bed, which was all good, except for the obvious problem.

"Sweetheart, I would love to take this back to your place, but I have a feeling I won't make my curfew," I admitted.

"Yeah, that could be a problem. Then again, I *am* your doctor and I *can* call the halfway house and tell them you'll be doing overnight outpatient work with me. Would you like that?"

I began moving inside her slowly again, to show her how much I liked that.

"Would *you* like that?" I whispered in her ear, gently sucking her earlobe.

"Ohhh, yeah, I'd like that," she moaned, passionately.

"Then let's go," I said, reluctantly pulling out of her and helping her down off the desk. We both dressed quickly, smiling at each other the entire time. Once we were presentable enough to step out in public, I took her hand and we headed out the door.

"You're not gonna regret this in the morning, are you?" I asked, seriously.

"If I thought that was a possibility, I wouldn't have let this happen tonight. Don't get me wrong, I understand the risk, because this relationship would be viewed as completely inappropriate by anyone who knows about it, but I'm not worried because I know you won't say anything. Your life is built around guarding your secrets, and that's what I do for a living, so we're kinda perfect for each other."

"I couldn't agree with you more," I replied, kissing her hand as we walked up the hallway to the front door. Once she had her office locked up tight, we made our way outside in companionable silence. And then all hell broke loose.

"Freeze, Mathis! Hands in the air!" A voice demanded. I looked up to find a cop approaching me from the left and the right, guns out in front of them with deadly intentions clear in their eyes.

"Officers, what did he do?" Su'Ryah asked, more confused than frightened.

"Ma'am, step away from him and keep your hands where we can see them," the cop closest to her ordered.

Immediately, my mind went to the gun in her purse and I saw this night ending completely different than what we planned.

"It's okay, Su'Ryah, do as they say," I encouraged.

"Officers, I'm Dr. Su'Ryah Davenport and Mr. Mathis is my patient, so I demand to know what he did wrong," she said, defiantly stepping in front of me, and becoming the target for their guns.

"Ma'am, for your own safety, *step away* from him. He may have already killed one woman tonight."

ARYANNA

Chapter 9

"We can sit here all night, or you can tell me what I want to know," Lieutenant Lake said again.

"Lawyer," I repeated, for what felt like the millionth time. In the last hour I'd been sitting in the First District police station, I'd asked for a lawyer to *every* question the cops sent at me, which should've ruled their interrogation over. The problem with law enforcement was that they believed they were above the law *and* my rights, but they still couldn't force me to talk, and I was smart enough to know talking wasn't in my best interest. The cop sitting across from me was black, stocky, and aggressive, which meant he was probably their go-to for intimidation and confessions. I wasn't new to this though.

"Look, we know you killed your daughter's mom, someone saw you in the area. Tell me what happened and I'll tell the district attorney you cooperated," Lake said.

"Law-yer!" I replied, smiling.

I knew they didn't really have shit. because if they did I would've been hooked and booked by now. Someone may have seen me around, but witness identification without an adequate line-up was easy to get tossed out of court, not to mention it was weak circumstantial evidence at best. Any real evidence they had went up in smoke with three-fourths of Jerika's apartment building, so I knew they were fishing.

"Help yourself, Mathis, because right now you're looking at first-degree murder, with at least thirty additional counts of attempted murder for those tenants you put in danger when you started that fire."

"I'm looking for a lawyer right now, and you're about to be looking for a new job," I countered, still smiling.

When Lt. Lake reached across the metal table between us and grabbed me by my suit jacket, I kept right on smiling, because now I knew I would get to whoop his ass without legal repercussions.

"I advise you to let go of my client, Lieutenant, unless you wanna pay for more than his dry cleaning bill," a female voice said, from over my shoulder.

He immediately let me go and I turned to find an attractive, cocoa-complexioned black woman standing there with the door open. She couldn't have been more than five feet six inches with her heels and Afro included, but the hawk look in her dark brown eyes said you could fuck with her at your own risk. I didn't know who she was, but I liked her already.

"And you are?" Lt. Lake asked, clearly unhappy.

"Monique Davenport, attorney for Mr. Mathis."

"Uh-huh. Well, I guess I'll give you a minute with your client," he replied, standing up.

"There's no need for that, Lieutenant, my client is free to go at this time. Oh, but you might want to take a minute and visit your captain once we leave, because I think he's anxious to speak with you. Let's go, Delontae," she said, stepping aside for me to walk out of the open door.

I knew better than to ask *any* type of questions, so I got my black ass up and got on the good foot.

"Thanks for getting me out," I said, once we were in the hallway.

"You can thank my cousin. For now, just keep your mouth shut and walk fast," she ordered.

My compliance was automatic, and five minutes after we picked up my property from one of the cops at the window. I was in the waiting area, coming face-to-face with Su'Ryah.

"Thank you," I said, pulling her into my arms and squeezing her tightly.

"Uh, I thought he was your patient," Monique commented.

"Not now, Nique. Are you okay?" Su'Ryah asked, looking up at me.

"I'm good. Sadly, I've been through all of that before," I replied, truthfully.

"What did you tell them?" Monique asked.

"Nothing, I ain't no rookie," I replied, slightly offended.

"Oh good, so then you know what happens next, right?" Monique asked.

"Yeah, they ain't got shit on me because I didn't do nothing. Me being in the area ain't shit, considering my daughter's cousin lives around there, and I dropped her off before hooking back up with Su'Ryah," I replied.

"Hooking up, huh?"

"I said, not *now,* Monique," Su'Ryah said, giving her cousin a nasty look.

"Okay whatever, but for you not being a rookie, you still obviously don't know how this game goes. Any contact with law enforcement for *any* reason is grounds for a technical violation of your probation," Monique informed me.

Now it was my turn to look at her with a nasty look.

"They can violate me for not doing shit except getting harassed by the police? No *way* that holds up in court," I replied, confidently.

"It ain't about it holding up in court, it's about them *holding you.* On a violation, you only go to the jail long enough for the transport van to come get you, and then it's off to prison until your court date. You already know that's a three to six month wait at best, and you won't get bail because of your criminal history," Monique concluded.

"So wait, he can go back to prison for *absolutely nothing?*" Su'Ryah asked, in complete disbelief.

"Our tax dollars at work, but it's not a question of *can* he go back to prison. He will," Monique said, with certainty.

"How do you know that?" I asked, looking around in anticipation of seeing a cop approaching with handcuffs.

"We need to finish this conversation elsewhere," Monique replied, heading for the front door.

Su'Ryah took my hand and we followed her out to the parking lot.

"Okay, so to answer your question, I know you're gonna be violated because the captain told me. The only reason he did that is because they already knew they can't pin the murder or the fire on you. You were just the easiest suspect, and your P.O. doesn't like you. Add that to the fact that your own process rights were violated, and you can see why they had to let you go tonight, but come tomorrow morning they're coming for you again," Monique stated.

"But *why?*" Su'ryah asked, angry and confused.

"Because they can. Because they feel like he's responsible for what happened to his baby mama, and they're hoping to keep him on ice until they can prove it, or he fucks up on the inside in a way that activates his back-up time. You see him as a person, but to the system, he'll always be a number or a piece to be controlled on life's chess board," Monique replied, truthfully.

The look on Su'Ryah's face after hearing her cousin's words was somewhere between bewilderment and utterly lost. I knew all too well the truth in what Monique said, because I'd been dealing with it since I was twelve years old, but that didn't make it any easier to hear. I knew two things for certain though. I couldn't win no fight against the government, and I needed to get far away from this police station.

"S-so what can he do, what can you do for him?" Su'Ryah asked.

Her question made her cousin look at me, and not even the surrounding darkness could hide the truth in her eyes.

"Thank you," I said, extending my hand for her to shake.

"You're welcome," Monique replied, sadly, shaking my hand.

"Su'Ryah, I want you to call me later, after you drop Delontae off."

I could tell Su'Ryah wanted to ask her cousin more question, but Monique quickly climbed into her car, leaving us standing there.

"Can you take me back to my car?" I asked.

"Of course," Su'Ryah replied, slowly.

We got into her car and left the police station parking lot, but I could tell by the tension-filled silence that we hadn't left the conversation behind.

"I just don't *understand*," Su'Ryah said, shaking her head.

"I got my first official charge when I was twelve years old, a gun charge, but you probably know that since you have access to my criminal files. That wasn't my first crime though. I started stealing when I was a kid, because I was hungry, and that turned into me stealing just because I could. I got away with it for the most part, but the first time the cops brought me home to my mom was for kicking in someone's front door and stealing a can of soda, and fifty dollars. I was ten years old. My mom beat my ass, and I thought it was for the obvious reasons of breaking the law and the cops having to bring me home, but I was wrong. She beat my ass because I'd gotten caught and added an irreversible strike to my life. Even though she did plenty of dirt, she understood that being a young, black man caught up in the judicial system was a life sentence, or in reality a death sentence. She didn't want that for me, so the lesson she wanted to teach in the moment was *don't get caught*. We both know I didn't learn that, and it's because the streets taught me that sometimes you had to get caught to make the proper lasting statement. What I *did* learn from my mother and my experiences that night is that the judicial system takes and doesn't give back. There *is* no way out, not even when you've paid your debt to society. Once you're locked up, you're a lifer, period."

"Don't say that, Delontae, because when you talk like that, you sound like those who've been defeated by their time. I know you're stronger than that, I know you're *smarter* than that," she replied, emphatically.

"Sweetheart, I'm also a realist, and you heard what your cousin just said back there. I could be in jail by tomorrow morning."

My words left her silent as she navigated the city that was still crawling with people and cars even at this late hour. To her way of thinking, I was accepting defeat by admitting what life was like for statistics like me. But to me, defeat would be allowing myself to wake up to handcuffs in the morning. I couldn't go out like that, so I spent the rest of the ride to her office, trying to formulate a plan in my mind. Twenty minutes later, I was still only able to come up with one solution.

"So, what are you gonna do?" she asked, once we were parked next to my car.

"Do you really wanna know?"

"What type of question is that? Do you really not understand that I care about you on a personal level now?" she asked, obviously hurt.

"That's not what I'm saying, Su'Ryah. I'm asking because I care about you too, and I want you to have plausible deniability."

"That sounds ominous, Delontae, what are you planning to do?"

I could see the fear and uncertainty clearly in her eyes, and it made me feel something I couldn't easily define or describe. I wasn't used to someone caring about me, at least not for anything other than selfish reasons.

"The only thing I can do is run, because I'm not going back inside. Not for three months, six months, or even one day. I'm *not*," I replied, emphatically.

"You can't do that, running will make it worse and you know that."

"How much worse does it get than going to prison for *no reason*? And no offense, but you've never had to walk in my shoes, despite coming from similar mud as me. I still have nightmares," I admitted, softly.

Su'Ryah wasn't like any woman I'd ever known. But she was, in the respect that she assumed like a lot of people did, that just because I'd survived prison and dominated in most ways, I came out on top. When you were really 'bout that life, I mean *really* doing dirt to people who may or may not have deserved it, it affected you. Even those of us who sold our souls had a price to pay in the end.

"Delontae, there has to be another way," she replied, distressed.

"Sweetheart, I wish there was. Believe me when I tell you that I'm *not* looking forward to leaving you, when I feel like I had to endure a lifetime of hell to get you," I said, genuinely, taking her hand in my own and looking deep into her blue eyes. When she leaned over to kiss me, I tasted more than lust on her tongue, and it tugged heavily on my heart, making me question my decision.

"I'm sorry," I whispered, against her soft lips.

"I know. Just like I know that if you're determined to leave, there's nothing I can say or do to change your mind, but will you allow me to make one last request?"

"Yes," I replied.

"I know you're not going back to the halfway house obviously. Spend the night with me," she said, looking me directly in the eye.

I felt my heartbeat in my throat and my mouth went dry in a way it hadn't since I was an inexperienced preteen, learning how to French kiss.

"I-I don't think it's a smart idea for me to be at your house or around you when my name hits the wanted streets."

"We don't have to go to my house, and I'll take my chances being around you. Just get in your car and follow me," she instructed.

My hesitation wasn't because I didn't wanna spend more time with her, I just didn't want to fuck up her life after she'd worked so hard to get where she was.

"I'm gone by sunrise," I said.

"Agreed," she replied, giving me a quick kiss before pulling back.

I got out of her car and slid behind the wheel of mine, and we got back on the road. Three hours later, we pulled into the parking lot of a DoubleTree hotel, just outside of Rockville, Maryland. I waited in my car while she went and got a room, and once I received her text, I made my way into the building to meet her. I kept my eyes straight ahead and walked with purpose, while still observing everyone and everything around me from the lobby to the seventh floor. As soon as I stepped off the elevator, I saw her standing in the hallway with the room door open, smiling nervously. When I got to her, I scooped her up into my arms and carried her inside the room, kicking the door shut behind us.

"Tell me what you want," I said, laying her gently on the bed.

"I want you to make sure I never forget you," she replied, sensually.

Those were the last words spoken until sunrise. We spent the hours in between coming together, changing positions and exchanging love faces, while creating memories that would make our bodies tingle long after this night. Neither of us wanted the moment to end, but being greedy could have disastrous results for both of us.

"Will you keep in touch?" she asked, laying her hand on my chest.

"There's no way I couldn't. I'll need my therapy sessions now more than ever, even though I'll be on the move constantly."

"I'll always be your doctor, and I'm here for you no matter where you are. Remember that."

Chapter 10

Four days later

The decision to leave the metropolitan area had been an easy one to make, but deciding where to go was a harder one. The world had changed dramatically in the two decades I'd been gone, making me feel like a goldfish trying to navigate the Atlantic Ocean. I was feeling an incredible amount of pressure to choose the right place to take refuge, since running had made my situation worse than it might've been if I'd stayed. And if that wasn't enough stress on my life, the fact that I could only comfort my daughter through Facebook posts had me feeling incredibly guilty. I wanted desperately to be there for her, especially considering how much of her life I'd already missed because of the bad decisions I'd made. Luckily for me, she wasn't listening to anyone trying to convince her that I'd killed her mom, and she would rather have me on the run than sitting in a cell again. Her understanding made me feel unworthy of her love, and I had absolutely no idea how to fix my dissolving relationship with her. Before I figured that out, I had to find somewhere to lay low, because the fact that I felt like every pair of eyes was watching me had my brain scattered.

After being on the move for four days, I realized I was unconsciously heading in the direction of one of the few people I believed in when it came to human decency. It felt like a lifetime ago when Su'Ryah asked me about a girlfriend and the need for companionship, but her question had pulled a face from my memory from my days of incarceration. I hadn't mentioned a word to Su'Ryah about it then, because I'd already made up my mind about never to bother the woman I was thinking of now, but times had changed. I was justifying my decision with practicalities like needing somewhere to hide where no one would think to look, and needing someone to help me who showed up nowhere in my history. Both of these things were true, but as the miles between us grew smaller, her face became clearer in my mind, and with that came the flood of memories that her and I shared.

Shawndra was a woman I'd loved once upon a time, but she was also someone I'd hurt, which meant helping me could be the last thing she wanted to do. As I drove past a sign that informed me I was now entering the city limits of Madison, Wisconsin, I knew I'd find out soon enough if Shawndra would help me like I hoped, or hurt me like I deserved. I made sure to stick to the speed limit while cruising through town, because I'd come *too* far to find myself in the clutches of the cops out here. Part of me wished I'd contacted Shawndra before I'd made the journey way up here, but the other part of me had let the fear of instant rejection rule that idea out. If she slammed the door in my face, my only other plan of action was to head out west. Su'Ryah told me she had family out there, but I was hesitant to involve her or her family in any more of my bullshit. Following the navigation provided by my car's GPS, I pulled up in front of Shawndra's house ten minutes later, feeling the same nervousness I had when I walked into Su'Ryah's office for the first time. Looking at the darkened duplex had me curing my luck, until I remembered something from our past. It was Tuesday night, which meant she was at her weekly Narcotic's Anonymous meeting. In her past life, pills and meth had been her demons, but she'd beat them back like a boss bitch should, and now she lived a dedicated sober existence. I respected her journey and I thought her strength was one of the sexiest things about her. A lot of people judged addicts, but where I came from, three out of four of your closest family members were addicted to one substance or another. We didn't judge them, we loved them. I pulled out my phone and did a search for the closest NA meeting, figuring she wouldn't go far from home, and the name Monona Serenity group popped up. It might've been smarter to wait here for her to return, than showing up in a public place as a newly wanted fugitive, but an argument could also be made for approaching her in public to lessen the tension and awkwardness. Plus, I really wasn't trying to put her in a weird position if she came home with a guy. If my memory served me correctly, she was definitely stingy with the pussy, but she was also a free white woman who could do what she pleased.

With my decision made, I put my car in gear and made the five-minute drive to the NA meeting location. It took a few minutes to gas myself up enough to get out of the car, but eventually I did it. I had no idea what other activities were going on inside the building, but the parking lot was packed, which made me feel better about my chances of blending in. I was walking towards the front door when movement in my peripheral vision caught my attention, and the sounds of a struggle piqued my curiosity. Suddenly, what was happening became clear.

"Get the fuck off me!" a female voice screamed.

I hadn't heard distress like that in a long time, but it was the familiarity of the voice that sent me into a dead sprint. I rounded the corner of the building to find a man pinning a woman to the side of it by her wrists, while he used his other hand to pull at the buttons on her shorts. Despite the darkness of the location, the attack was definitely a bold one, but mine would be bolder. Just as calmly as I'd order food from a drive-thru, I stepped up behind the man and snapped his neck mercilessly, tossing his body to the ground like a used condom. Her eyes immediately met mine, and the change from fear and anger to instant recognition made my heart beat faster.

"It-it's you. You're here," Shawndra said, slowly, in obvious disbelief.

"I'm here, but we gotta go," I replied, reaching for her hand.

If I expected our reunion to be that smooth, I should've remembered who I was dealing with, and then maybe I would've ducked. I didn't though, and her slap to my face ricocheted loudly across the parking lot like a gunshot.

"Where the fuck have you *been*? How could you just disappear on me like that, after all the promises you made, after all the shit I've been through with you? And what about my *kids*, did you forget all the promises you made them about the future and us being a family, you asshole? I *trusted* you, I believed every goddamn lie you told me and—"

"Shawndra!" I yelled, grabbing her by the shoulders to stop her tirade. "You have every right to be mad, but given the fact that there's a dead man literally inches from us, do you think we can finish the conversation somewhere else," I suggested, as calmly as I could.

I remembered her eyes as being green, but right now they were shooting red flames at me. I wasn't into putting my hands on women, despite having made easy work of the six foot, two-hundred-pound mufucka trying to attack her, I was worried she was gonna try to fight me, and I'd have my hands full. Shawndra was five-eight, two hundred pounds of beauty, with long brown hair highlighted with blond streaks, but she was a fighter in every sense of the word. She had to be or life would've swallowed her long before now, and I respected that about her. I just didn't want to fight with her. She glanced at the dead guy and then back at me.

"Let me go," she demanded, in a voice that was calmer, but still hostile.

I took my hands off her, while also taking a step back because mama didn't raise no fool.

"I'm assuming you have a car if you made it this far," she stated.

"I do."

"Good, you can follow me, but don't think for a *second* we're not finishing this conversation," she replied, walking away.

As I made my way back to my car, there was a part of me that said, *get in and get the fuck out of town*. Not just because I'd been here less than half an hour and had *already* killed a mufucka, but because it was obvious, I'd hurt Shawndra deeply, and that had me feeling like shit. The other part of me knew that even if I was gonna leave, I'd come too far to do it without giving her some type of explanation. At the very least I owed her that. Once I was behind her white SUV, I was basically following her on autopilot because my mind was traveling through time and space back to where we'd begun. Some would call it luck how her and I came to be, but there was no way that was all it added up to in my mind. While it was true, I'd first seen her on Facebook, the fact that I only had access to Facebook because I'd been transferred to a different prison where it was easier to buy a cellphone couldn't be ignored. Neither could the circumstances surrounding that particular transfer, because it was actions five years in the making that had led to that move. To my way of thinking, it was only divine intervention that had brought us together. From the very first time I'd seen her picture, there was something that drew me to her, and it went deeper than just how attractive she was. At the time, I'd been in a *more than* complicated relationship, so I couldn't step to her, but I'd watched and waited, learning all I could about her from a distance. Finally, not even that was enough, and I'd had to create an alter ego on Facebook, so I could holla at her without my current entanglement knowing. Looking back now, I still felt some shame for all the lies I'd told Shawndra in the beginning, but the memory of how she'd reacted to the truth made me smile. Most women would've run the opposite way when I divulged my criminal past, but Shawndra had offered me a clean slate and all the love my heart could handle. She quickly became my backbone, my number one woman and someone I couldn't see myself living without. We made so many plans, but fear forced me to try and forget those plans. Not because I wanted to, but because I had to. Our lives weren't oil and water, they were *blood* and water, and my conscience wouldn't allow those two to mix.

Us pulling into the parking lot of a Holiday Inn Express brought my trip down memory lane to a halt. I watched her get out of her truck and signal for me to wait where I was while she disappeared into the hotel. Within a few minutes she was back outside waving me in, so I turned off my car, pulled the hood up on my black hoodie, and got out. Before leaving the hotel room with Su'Ryah in Maryland, she'd insisted I take her gun with me, and it crossed my mind not to retrieve it from under the driver's seat, but I wanted to feel Shawndra out first. We walked into the hotel, appearing to be just like any other couple, and made our way to room four-twenty-four without incident. I hadn't been nervous walking through the lobby or in the elevator, but once we got behind closed doors, I could feel my palms sweating.

"Who was that guy?" I asked, immediately going on the offensive.

"Why the fuck do you care? I'm obviously not your *wife* anymore," she replied, hostility.

"I care because the mufucka was about to rape you. And if you're not my wife, why do you still have on the ring I bought you?"

I watched closely as her eyes unconsciously went to her ring finger before flickering back up to me. We technically weren't married on paper, but that was how we'd viewed our relationship before I disappeared months ago. I had proposed, and seeing the ring I'd done it with still on her finger was stirring up old emotions.

"You don't have the right to question me about anything, not until you explain why I hadn't heard from you in six months," she retorted, taking a seat on one of the two beds in the room.

I sat down across from her, trying to organize my thoughts and the words to explain my behavior.

"First of all, I'm sorry. I know that's not gonna make up for any of the pain I've caused, but from the bottom of my heart, I'm truly sorry. The reason I've been out of touch is because when I got transferred back to my original prison in preparation for my release, I found out just how real the threats were from my old lifestyle. I changed, you know I changed, but some people couldn't remember how to forget, and I knew there would be drama once I got out. I told you a long time ago, I wouldn't bring that near you or the kids."

"And I told you to just bring your ass *here*! You didn't have to go back to the drama in D.C., We'd made a home a home for you *here*," she replied, emotionally.

"I had to do ninety days in a halfway house, babe, so I couldn't just leave."

"You could've *told* me that though, Delontae. I waited years for you, don't you think I would've waited three more fucking months? Stop giving me bullshit excuses and just tell me why you intentionally hurt me like that, because I didn't deserve it."

"No, you didn't. But I didn't deserve you. Shawndra, I'm not giving you bullshit excuses. I'm being all the way real with you, and I'm telling you I didn't want you or your kids hurt by my past decisions. I care about you way too much for that," I replied, genuinely.

"If that's true, then what's changed? Your past is still your past, yet here you are, and from the way you just handled that situation back there, you're not worrying about breaking the law."

"Shawndra, he was trying to *rape you* and I—"

"And you could've stopped him without killing him, but you didn't, did you? Let me ask you something, Delontae, when did you get out?"

"Almost two months ago," I replied slowly, avoiding her penetrating stare.

"That means you haven't finished your time at the halfway house, yet here you are in good old Wisconsin, saving me. I thank you for that, but I'm wondering if I'm looking at the man I fell in love with, or 'The Lion' he was supposed to have left behind," she said, thoughtfully.

I didn't have a response that wouldn't sound like bullshit to my own ears, so I decided to keep my mouth shut. I'd expected to run into an emotional tirade, but her logical side seemed to be winning out against emotion, and that could make shit worse for me.

"Why are you here, Delontae?" she asked, pointedly.

"That's a long story."

"Check out time isn't until eleven a.m. so we've got plenty of time, and don't you *dare* look at me like that, because sex is *not* an option," she stated, emphatically.

I couldn't hide my smile, not just because of the comment she'd made, but because of the memories of the wild-ass phone sex we used to have that were currently flooding my mind. Common sense said that right now was probably *the worst* time to take that trip down memory lane, so instead I started explaining the last couple months of my life. Of course, I had to omit certain details about my interactions with Rahsheeda and Su'Ryah, but I kept it funky about everything else that had happened. One thing I'd always loved about Shawndra was the fact that she didn't judge me, even though she knew the things I was capable of. Other than Su'Ryah, no woman had ever been able to do that.

We stayed up talking well past sunrise, finally getting around to her and the guy I'd killed, as well as touching on everything that had been happening in her life. I'd missed so much, but even more than that, I'd missed her. I thought I'd been doing the right thing by trying to forget her love, but sitting here talking, sharing the same air, and breathing in the sweet smell of her skin for the first time in years had me feeling different.

"So now you're on the run, what's next?" she asked.

"I don't really know. I'll probably head out west and hide out with Su'Ryah's people."

"How about we call her Dr. Davenport, because that's what she is, your former doctor. And I don't think it's a good idea for you to put so much trust into somebody you just met, because you *know* that never ends well for you," she replied.

"Okay, so what are you saying?"

"I'm saying you know you can trust me. I'm saying no more bullshit, no more lies, and no more running. You promised me a future, and now you're keeping that promise. You're mine."

Chapter 11

One week later

"Come on, James!" I yelled, smiling like every other proud parent sitting in the bleachers of the little league game.

Right now, Shawndra's thirteen-year-old son was up to bat, and I couldn't explain the joy I was feeling at finally getting to see him play. This moment had been planned years ago, but the actual experience was beyond what I'd imagined.

"Eye on the ball, come on, buddy," Shawndra yelled, encouraging him.

He swung at the first pitch and missed, but we were still yelling encouragements at him. When the second pitch hit him in the back, my smile vanished and I was immediately on my feet, ready to sprint onto the field and whoop the pitcher's ass. It didn't matter that the pitcher was another little kid. I was prepared to beat his ass and then his parents.

"Delontae, don't!" Shawndra said, grabbing my hand in a firm grip.

"I just wanna make sure he's good," I replied, pulling away, and making my way down to the fence behind home plate so I could get a better look. Of course, she followed me to make sure I stayed true to my word, which was a good thing for the pitcher and his family. The even better thing was that James was already jogging to first base, and he appeared to be fine.

"See, he's okay, it happens sometimes," Shawndra said, taking my hand and interlocking our fingers as we both kept a close eye on the game.

I tried to will my body not to shake in anger, but I could still feel a slight tremble.

"I'm just glad he's good," I replied.

"Me too, but even if he wasn't, it's not okay for you to do what you were about to do."

"What are you talking about?" I asked, innocently.

"You're forgetting that I know you, which mean something I know you were getting ready to go have a word with that pitcher, and probably his family too. *Not okay*, Delontae, especially not when you're supposed to be keeping a low profile. There's no room for 'The Lion' in Madison, Wisconsin, understand?"

Everything in me wanted to call her analysis complete bullshit, but I'd agreed not to lie to her anymore.

"Fine," I said, reluctantly and through gritted teeth.

We both stood there and watched while the next batter up hit a fly ball that ended the game. While we waited on James to go through the customary good sportsmanship things, I pulled Shawndra aside.

"I'm sorry, I know I was about to overreact, but I'm protective," I said.

"I understand that, but you know that you can't react with violence out here in the real world. This isn't prison, you're gonna have to tell The Lion to sit, babe."

I was just about to say something smart when I saw James round the gate and spot me.

"Delontae!" he yelled, running full speed at me and leaping into my arms. I was thankful he was small for his age because he had enough momentum behind him to knock me down. Still, it warmed my heart that he was so excited to see me.

"When did you get here?" he asked, with a huge smile lighting up his face.

"I saw your whole game, buddy, and you were great," I replied.

"Yeah, but we still lost."

"It's okay, don't be discouraged. Sometimes you win, sometimes you lose, but both are good excuses for ice cream," I replied, winking at him.

"Mom, can we go for ice cream?" James asked, looking at Shawndra expectantly.

"Nice going," she mumbled, under her breath.

"Uh, I don't know buddy, we have to ask—"

"James, come here," a man's voice suddenly demanded.

I knew Shawndra had been about to say they had to go ask her ex-husband, the father to both of her kids, but he'd obviously found us first. I wasn't surprised though, so I put James back on his feet so he could go to the man standing a few feet away. I noticed Shawndra's daughter, Marie, standing a little behind her dad with an ugly chick I could only assume was his new wife. He'd definitely downgraded.

"William, do you think it would be okay for us to take the kids out for ice cream?" Shawndra asked.

"We? Who's he?"

"That's Delontae, Dad, Mom's—"

"Go stand with your sister and Lisa," William said to James, never taking his eyes away from Shawndra's face.

I could see the disappointment on James's face and it brought my anger back instantly.

"This is my fiancé, Delontae," Shawndra replied, taking my hand in hers.

"Your fiancé? I didn't even know you had a *boyfriend.*"

"Is that really your business?" I asked, calmly.

"It's my business to know who's around my children," William replied, somewhat aggressively.

Shawndra immediately squeezed my hand and I knew that was her way of telling me not to overreact, not to introduce this smug sumbitch to "The Lion." I understood the validity of his concerns, but right now I was remembering everything Shawndra had told me about their ten-year marriage, and the years since the divorce. I didn't like this mufucka, not even a little.

"As you can see, your son knows who I am, and I'm betting Marie's reaction to me would be the same if she were allowed to come over here. I mean neither of them any harm, I love them as much as I do my own daughter," I replied, in the same calm tone.

"Love them? You don't even *know* them! Shawndra, I don't know what the fuck you're trying to pull, but—"

"Don't talk to her like that," I warned in a deadly whisper, taking a step towards him.

"Delontae, don't. William, he just wants to take them to get ice cream and then we'll bring them straight home, I promise," Shawndra said.

I could see the fear in her eyes, and it was slowly nourishing the animal inside me that wanted to pull his head off so I could shit down his throat. For Shawndra's sake, I kept the leash on the animal.

"N-no, it's too late for ice cream. Besides, if you can afford ice cream, you can afford to give me the little money I expect from you for child support," he replied, in an unsteady voice.

We all knew he was being petty for even saying some shit like that, especially considering that Dairy Queen would only cost a few dollars. I was the king of petty though.

"Are you referring to that fifty dollars a month she gives you?" I asked, already reaching into my pocket.

He couldn't hide the look of surprise on his face about me knowing their business, but he would've *really* been fucked up if I would've brought up his dick size, the fact she took his virginity, or how bad he was in bed. Because the kids weren't far away, I chose to keep it cute.

"William, you know I'm gonna give you the money, I just didn't have a chance to take it out before we got here," Shawndra said.

"Preoccupied with other things, no doubt," he remarked, smartly.

The sound of his voice was starting to make my skin crawl, but I maintained my composure nonetheless.

"Let's see, fifty dollars a month times twelve months is, here, babe, pass this six hundred to little Willie. I mean, William. That should cover the next year," I said, counting the money out and giving it to Shawndra.

I could tell she was fighting a losing battle against her smile, just like I could tell that William was pissed enough to wanna make a bad decision. The look I leveled at him made it clear that not only would that be a decision he'd immediately regret, but I'd *enjoy* making him regret it. He was smart enough to take the money though, and quickly walk away from us.

"James and Marie, we love you, and we'll see you this weekend," Shawndra hollered.

They both shook their heads, but I could see the sadness in their eyes, and it angered me again.

"So, that's William, huh? I thought he would be taller," I said, smiling tightly at Shawndra.

"You're so *bad*! Come on," she replied, pulling me in the direction of her truck.

"I thought I was being good actually, because we *both* know how I wanted to handle that asshole."

"Yeah, I know, but he's still my kids' dad. I do appreciate you not doing anything in front of the kids, I mean, other than make William look like a complete ass," she replied, laughing.

It was good to see her relaxed so quickly after that tense situation, and it went a long way toward soothing the savage in me. I had no doubt that William and I would have our day though, because he wasn't smart enough not to ruffle my feathers.

"So, do you want to get ice cream?" I asked, opening the driver side door of her truck and helping her in, before going around to the passenger side.

"We could order some from room service."

"You sure you wanna go back to the hotel with me?" I asked.

"Do you not want me to go?"

"You know better than that. I only asked because you ain't been home all week. I feel like I've blown into town and dominated your life," I replied, honestly.

"Okay, you act like that's a bad thing. It's not like you kidnapped me or I haven't been going to work, I just haven't been home. I can go home if you want though, because I think this is really about us still sleeping in separate beds," she said, smiling as she started the truck and pulled off.

I opened my mouth to counter the shot she'd just taken, but she got spared by my ringing phone. When I finally got it out of my pocket, the smile on my face froze as I saw who was calling me. I knew if I answered the call, shit would definitely get real awkward, but to not answer it would seem more than a little suspicious to Shawndra.

"Hello?"

"Hey stranger, I ain't heard from you in a few days and I just wanted to make sure you're okay," Su'Ryah said.

"I'm good, just staying out of the way. Are you alright?"

"You mean, aside from the fact that I'm missing you more than I ever have any man? Yeah, I'm good. This is a weird feeling," she admitted.

"How so?" I asked, feeling Shawndra's gaze swing in my direction.

"I didn't expect to care this much about you and now that you're gone, I'm not sure what to do with these feelings. I don't want them to go away, just like I didn't want you to go away. I don't know how to change the situation you're in though, Delontae," she replied, sounding tired.

"I don't know what to do either, I wasn't expecting things to play out the way they have. Have you heard from Monique?"

"She doesn't know anything more than there's a warrant out for your arrest for a probation violation, and they're still investigating Jerika's death."

"Any clues about where I might be hiding?" I asked, glancing at Shawndra out of the side of my eye.

"Not that I've heard. I'm feeling some type of way that you won't tell though. I thought you trusted me."

"Don't do that, because you know I'm only trying to give you plausible deniability. Just let shit calm down a little," I insisted.

"I guess I don't have a choice, but keep in mind that I have some vacation time I'm planning to take, and we're meeting up. I'm not taking no for an answer."

I could feel the temperature rising in the truck's confines, and I knew that heat was coming from Shawndra. I needed to end this call before she started voluntarily biting a hole in her tongue.

"That's fine, but we can talk about that when the time comes? You know we shouldn't stay on the phone too long."

"I know. Just don't go days without calling me, I worry," she admitted softly.

"I'm sorry. I'll be in touch soon," I said, disconnecting the call.

Shawndra didn't immediately speak or look at me, but there was no doubt in my mind what was coming.

"So, who was that?" she asked.

"You know who that was, don't play games."

"What did she want?" Shawndra asked, calmly.

"I haven't called in a while so she wanted to check in and update me on what's going on."

"Why do I feel like that's not all she wanted? Have you told me everything about you and her, Delontae?"

"Is there any woman you think I'm *not* fucking?" I countered, smoothly dodging her question.

"Hey you admitted to me a long time ago that you were a whore, so I have the right to ask questions."

"I *was* a whore, past tense, but it seems like these days I'm celibate," I replied, giving her a knowing look.

"You'll stay that way if you're waiting on me to make a move," she said, under her breath.

I chose to act like I didn't hear her smart ass comment, but my mind was already working overtime. We rode the rest of the way to the hotel in silence, and I could tell she was still feeling some type of way about Su'Ryah. Most men looked at women in these situations as insecure, but I was smart enough to know that most insecure women were made that way by a nothing-ass nigga. I didn't wanna be that guy for Shawndra, she deserved so much better than that. I took her hand in mine as we pulled into the hotel parking lot, and I kissed each of her fingers before taking them individually into my mouth and sucking on them slowly. I knew this would make her think about me sucking her sensitive nipples and her clit, and it would make her horny. I could hear the change in her breathing immediately and I knew I had her undivided attention, even though she wasn't looking at me.

"Come on," I said, opening my door after I'd completed my round of torture.

We both got out and met on the sidewalk, and I couldn't help smiling at how fast her hand ended up back in my own. Outwardly, I was playing it cool as we entered the hotel and made our way to our room, but on the inside I was nervous as shit! Shawndra wasn't any other woman to me, and she wasn't some random chick. At one point in time, she was the woman I'd envisioned spending the rest of my life with, so sex was never just looked at like *sex*, it was making love. I didn't have a lot of experience with making love, but both the gangsta and the gentleman in me wanted to experience it with her.

"I'm gonna order something from room service, do you want anything?" I asked, once we were in the room.

"No, I'm gonna take a shower since you used all the hot water earlier."

"*Whatever*," I replied, laughing.

When she disappeared into the bathroom, I placed my order, and asked for it to be rushed right up. I was still nervous, but I knew that what happened next would be more natural than anything I'd experienced. Within five minutes, a waiter was wheeling my requested provisions through the door, and quickly disappearing the way he'd come. I left the bottle of Mountain Dew chilling in the wine bucket, and the strawberries sitting on the tray, but I moved the bottle of whipped cream to the nightstand in between our beds. After dimming the lights, I made my clothes disappear faster than Clark Kent, and then I went in search of my woman.

"What are you doing?" she asked, startled by me pulling the shower door open without warning.

All it took was for her to take one look down and she knew *exactly* what I was about to do.

"Delontae, I—"

Whatever she was about to say was silenced by my mouth descending on hers, as I allowed all the hunger I felt for her to consume me. Our kisses were passionate, but not violent. They were thorough, while also seeking knowledge of one another. Falling deeper under her spell, my hands moved from her face so I could pull her close to me, as the need to feel her heated flesh grow with each passing moment. I don't know how long we stayed locked together under the water's spray, but the oral communication we were sharing was the realest I'd ever experienced in life.

"I n-need to be inside you," I whispered into her mouth, lifting her into my arms.

The animal in me wanted to pin her to the shower wall, but the need to take my time with her made me carry her out of the shower and to the bed. The sight of her naked beauty was breathtaking, and I drank it in from head to toe before laying down on top of her. My dick was already throbbing in anticipation, but this was about complete fulfillment and not momentary gratitude. Starting with her neck, I kissed my way from side to side, making sure to nibble on each earlobe during my travels, before moving lower and letting my lips walk along her collarbone. The sound of her labored breathing indicated her body was feeling the right things, and so my journey continued lower still across her breasts, pausing at her hard nipples. A flicker of my tongue over the sensitive gumdrop forced her back to arch a little, and her breath to halt in its escape from her mouth, which made me smile as I gave the other one equal attention. I took my time licking lazy circles around both nipples before pulling one, and then the other, in between my lips and sucking on them slowly.

With each passing moment, I could hear her body coming alive like the flickering flames of a fire that's destined to be an inferno. I was determined to make that fire rage. My journey of kisses continued down her stomach, slowly, yet with clear purpose and determination, until I arrived at the sweet center of her lollipop. My lips and tongue went to work on her clit, while my index finger took a walk inside her wetness. Just the feeling of how tight her pussy was had my dick howling for an introduction, and the gentleness of my touch had her back now arching off the bed.

"Delontae," she moaned, grabbing ahold of my dreadlocks like I was the last lifeboat on the *Titanic*. I quickly added another finger to the party, and allowed my hand and mouth to work in concert until the melody of her first climax echoed loudly in the room. I drank in her sweet nectar like it was sacramental wine capable of cleansing my soul, and only when I had enough did I start kissing my way back up her body. By the time I reached her soft hips, the look of hunger in her eyes was so pronounced that her pupils had dilated. I gave her gentle kisses while slowly pushing my dick inside her until nothing in the world separated us. She was still so incredibly tight and wet that I was forced to take a few deep breaths before setting a rhythm we could both vibe to. Each stroke mattered, meaning the deeper I pushed, the harder I fell for her, and I *loved* it. Everything in me was screaming for me to go faster, but I took my time until I felt her body begin to tremble.

"You ready?"

"Uh-huh," she moaned, working her pussy muscles in a way that hurt so good. The battle of wills began as the speed increased, but I didn't feel like we were fighting for dominance. We were fighting for forever. Suddenly, give and take turned into us both taking, and we came together in a symphony of moans and screams. I was so weak afterwards that I had to immediately lay next to her to keep from collapsing on top of her.

"That, that was, oh God that was…"

"Uh-huh," she replied, weakly, causing both of us to laugh.

I somehow managed to get us both underneath the covers and I became the big spoon to her little spoon. We stayed like that until sleep came calling.

Chapter 12

I opened my eyes to find myself staring at the back of Shawndra's head, with her still snuggled against me and I sighed with contentment, because what we'd shared hadn't been a dream. So many lonely nights in prison had been spent imagining this moment, but the real thing was so much better and too beautiful for words. I kissed her shoulder softly, causing her to stir a little, but she didn't wake up. My intention had been to let her sleep and rejoin her in the land of peaceful slumber, but now the taste of her skin on my tongue was giving me different ideas. We were both still laying on our left sides spooning, so I simply moved her right leg a little and slowly guided my dick back inside her. With my arms wrapped around her, I could feel the exact moment she came fully awake, because her heart started banging in her chest.

"It's just me, baby. I love you," I whispered, using my right hand to play with her nipples, while diving deeper into her tight wetness.

"I l-love you too," she moaned, matching me stroke for stroke and throwing that ass back at me. I made her body sing for me as I alternated between playing with her nipples and her clit, while increasing my speed until my thrusts turned into the pounding blows that would make her toes curl.

"Oh fuck!" she moaned loudly, before cumming with the intensity of a tropical storm. Feeling her rain on me only made me slam into her harder as aftershocks rocked her body's nerve endings.

I could feel her trying to force me to cum with her, but I had other plans. Without warning I pulled out of her, rolled her on her back, and grabbed the whipped cream off the nightstand.

"Wh-what are you doing?" she asked, breathlessly.

"Shhh, just enjoy," I replied, kneeling in between her legs and pulling them up around my neck.

From this angle, I was able to slide my dick back inside her while spraying whipped cream on her toes and licking it off. The dual sensations of having her toes sucked while getting long, slow strokes of good dick had her eyes bulging and her mouth wide open. It only took her another five minutes to reach heaven's gate again, and me switching feet pushed her through those gates headfirst.

"Babe, babe, I can't," she pleaded, shaking her head.

I kept right on sucking her whipped-cream-covered toes, loving how she couldn't stop her eyes from rolling to the back of her head, as the power of my strokes intensified. I was merciless with her, riding her hard for the longest half-hour of her life until we came together and collapsed, exhausted. We laid there side by side, watching the shadows move and change in the room as daylight beat the darkness away outside our room.

"God, my mouth is dry," she said, in a hoarse voice.

Her comment reminded me of the two-liter bottle of Mt. Dew I'd ordered the night before, forcing me to get up and retrieve it. I poured us both a champagne glass full of the cool green liquid, and returned to the bed with the tray of strawberries cradled in my arms.

"When did you do all this?" she asked, happily surprised.

"Last night, we just never got around to it."

"Yeah, because you were trying to fuck my brains out," she replied, smiling and accepting the glass I gave her.

"You loved it though, right?"

"Hell yeah! I mean, I knew it would be good, but damn!"

"I won't lie, you've got that come-back pussy," I said, laughing, sitting down next to her.

My comment made her blush, but I knew that was because by her own admission, her sex life had been boring to say the least. After what I'd experienced, I knew now it wasn't a problem with *her*.

"Uh, thank you, I guess," she replied, sheepishly.

"No babe, thank *you*," I said, covering a strawberry with whipped cream and feeding it to her.

I quickly licked the extra whipped cream from the corner of her mouth, thinking that another round of lovemaking was in short order. Unfortunately, my ringing phone meant my thirst for her body would have to wait.

"Who's calling you this early in the morning?" she asked, irritated.

"I don't know, but nothing this early can mean good news," I replied, reluctantly climbing out of bed and retrieving my phone from my pants pocket.

Seeing Su'Ryah's number brought my eyes immediately back to Shawndra's.

"Put it on speaker phone," she demanded seriously, knowing who the caller was.

The potential for disaster was clear to me, but the look on Shawndra's face told me this wasn't a request to be refused. When my phone stopped ringing before I could answer, I thought that I was off the hook, but only seconds passed before it started ringing again.

"Answer the phone, Delontae," Shawndra ordered, taking a drink from her glass.

I was boxed in and I knew it.

"What's wrong?" I asked, by way of answering the phone.

"Delontae?"

"I'm here, what's wrong?" I asked again.

"It's Maleah, she got arrested again."

"What? Why?" I asked, feeling panic and anger grip me at the same time.

"She was in the car with this guy and there was a gun found when they got pulled over. She swears it wasn't hers, but her family either doesn't believe her or doesn't care because they won't get her out. It was by sheer luck that she ran into my cousin, recognized the last name, and got a message to me. She needs you though."

"I'm on my way. I'll call you from the road, but I want you to meet me at the last place you saw me," I replied, hanging up and quickly putting my clothes on.

"Wait a minute, Delontae, you can't go back there," Shawndra said, hopping up out of bed and standing in front of me.

"I don't have a choice, my daughter needs me."

"What the hell are you gonna do besides get locked back up, or get yourself killed by going back down there? Going back doesn't make any sense."

"It doesn't have to make sense to you, Shawndra. This ain't about *you* right now," I replied frustrated, but not pausing in getting dressed.

"Wow, how can you say that? I'm not trying to make it all about me, but this decision you're making affects me because something can happen to you. That definitely affects me, *and* the kids."

"Don't do that. Don't try to make me feel guilty by bringing up James and Marie, like I'm supposed to choose between them and Maleah. That's not how you want this conversation to go," I warned, searching for my shoes.

"Delontae, I'm not trying to make you choose, I'm just trying to get you to make *good decisions*. I want you to help

Maleah, because I care about her too. I'll even give you the money to get her out of jail, and you can have her come up here."

"So then she can be on the run too? No, she's not gonna live her life like that, and there's no way D.C. would agree to let her leave their jurisdiction. A gun charge is serious, especially for the Feds, so the only way for me to truly help Maleah is to get her from under that," I explained.

"How though Delontae? You're going back there without a plan, which means shit can go wrong. You just need to slow down and think, not make impatient decisions."

I couldn't deny that she was kicking sound logic at me, but my decision wasn't based on logic alone. This was an emotional call, because this was my daughter we were discussing, the same daughter I hadn't done shit for in her entire life, because I'd been the definition of an absentee parent. I was making this decision based on all the promises I'd made her about doing anything in the world for her, if I'd only had the chance. Here was my chance.

"Baby, you have to trust me," I said, taking her face in my hands and kissing her softly.

Her eyes were bright with a fear she couldn't give words to, and the guilt it made me feel made it harder to leave. I had to do it though.

"I'll be back soon," I promised, kissing her again, and then heading for the door.

Aside from Maleah, it had never been hard for me to leave anyone before, but with each step I could feel Shawndra's love pulling me in the opposite direction I was headed. I wanted to go back to the hotel room we'd been sharing, take her in my arms, and make love to her until the world disappeared around us. Unfortunately, I couldn't do that. I couldn't go back, so I had to focus on what was in front of me. Once I got behind the wheel of my car and got on the road, I called Su'Ryah back.

"I'm on my way."

"How long will it take you to get here?" she asked.

I looked at the time on my phone.

"I should be there by two or three p.m."

"Delontae, that's damn near nine hours, where the fuck are you *coming* from?" she asked, clearly surprised by how far from home I traveled.

"Su'Ryah, don't start, just tell me what you know about Maleah," I replied, quickly.

"I told you everything already. Her bond is fifty thousand dollars, and the boy she was with already got out."

"Who the fuck is this nigga anyway?" I asked, glad to have a target to focus my anger on.

"Monique asked the same question when she went to see Maleah, but your daughter can be more evasive than you. All I know is he's some dude she's been kicking it with, and based on what happened, I think it's a safe assumption to say he's in the street."

I was hoping she was wrong about that, because no father wanted their daughter with a bad boy, especially not coming from where I came from. Sadly, I knew that square niggas weren't riding around with guns in their cars.

"Did they appoint Maleah a lawyer yet?" I asked.

"Monique took the case after I talked to her and let her know who Maleah was, so she's in good hands. She is concerned though."

"Is there a reason to be concerned, other than the obvious?" I asked, fighting against worry creeping up inside me.

"Well, Monique thinks if it comes out who Maleah's dad is, meaning you, she won't get anything like the benefit of doubt or a fair trial. Plus, it doesn't help that she was already out on bond."

I took a moment to process that information, looking for a way to minimize the damage.

"Has Monique looked into the lil nigga Maleah was with, because if he's really 'bout that life, he has to have skeletons in his closet," I said.

"I can tell her to do that. It there anything else you need me to do?"

"Do you feel comfortable bailing her out again, and I'll pay you back?" I asked, hopeful.

"Of course, I just didn't want to do anything without talking to you first. I'll have it done before you get here, and I'll bring her to the hotel with me."

"Nah, that's not a good idea, because they might have eyes on her hoping to find me. Even if it's not because of this situation she's in, I'm sure the homicide detectives working her mom's case are watching and waiting. So, I don't even want you to personally go bond her out yourself, just give Monique the money and let her handle it. Also, have Monique give you whatever info she has on the nigga Maleah was with, and whatever she don't know, you tell my daughter she better speak on it. I want to know who he is and where to find him," I replied, seriously.

"What are you gonna do?" Su'Ryah asked, slowly.

"Remember the things you can't ask, because they put you in bad situations," I replied, cryptically.

My comments left her silent, but I could still hear her breathing so I knew she was on the phone.

"I feel like I'm seeing a different side of you, maybe the side I've only read about in your files."

"I'm sorry if that changes how you see me, but—"

"It does change my view of you, but not how you think or how I would've suspected. You're not reckless or overly impulsive, you're determined. I thought it would be scary or off-putting to see you in your element, to see that strength you keep a tight leash on. It's not though, it's actually kind of sexy," she confessed.

Now it was her words that left me somewhat speechless, but I could feel the smile tugging at the corners of my mouth.

"I'm not sure what to say to that," I replied, honestly.

"There's nothing you need to say, I just wanted to tell you how I was feeling in the moment. I'll take care of your daughter and I'll see you when you get here. Drive safe, okay?"

"I will, and thank you so much, Su'Ryah. I can't put into words how much your support means to me."

"You just did," she replied, emotionally.

We disconnected our call and my focus swung to the road in front of me. Not just the one I was currently navigating, but the road I was preparing to go back down for my daughter. It was official now. The Lion was loose.

Chapter 13

"It's about time you got here," Su'Ryah said, leaping into my arms as soon as she opened the door.

"You know I had to do the speed limit, but I made it in one piece," I replied, sitting her down and closing the door.

"I'm just glad you're back."

"Update me on what's going on," I requested, moving further into the room and taking a seat on the queen-sized bed.

"Monique got Maleah out, but at the last minute, the magistrate insisted on house arrest. Nique figured somebody whispered your name in the judge's ear, but since her bond couldn't be taken away, they settled for an ankle monitor. She's at Monique's house now, and she wants to see you, but I told her you weren't in town."

"I wanna see her too, I just don't think that's a good idea. We'll figure that out later, for now I wanna know if she gave up all the details on old boy," I replied.

"Monique said *that* was an exercise in pulling teeth, but eventually Maleah folded. Apparently, they went to school together, before he dropped out to be a dope boy, and they've been kicking it for about six months now. His name is Keyshawn. He's nineteen years old, and he's from West Baltimore, Maryland, but he lives and works the corners in Southwest D.C."

"My daughter fucking this nigga?" I asked, hating the foul taste that question left in my mouth.

"Uh, I didn't ask all that, Delontae, and I don't think that's a question you really want the answer to. I know she ain't happy with the dude now, because he didn't handle the situation how a real man should."

"At least she's smart enough to realize that. Did you get everything I need?" I asked, looking around the room.

My question sent her to the closet behind the door and she returned with a duffle bag in her hand, passing it to me. I inventoried it quickly, taking out what I would need in the immediate future. After taking a sheet off of the bed, spreading it out on the floor, and putting a chair in the middle of it, I turned to Su'Ryah expectantly.

"You sure about this?" she asked, picking up the scissors off of the bed.

"It's only hair. Plus, I have no choice except to change my appearance."

I'd been growing my dreads for more than five years, and it had never been my intention to cut them, but I felt like they made me too easy to identify. My beard would have to be severely trimmed too.

"I love your hair though," she said, stroking it gently before grabbing a fistful of it.

"Don't worry, it doesn't change my swag. Just do it."

Twenty minutes later my head was lighter on my shoulders than it had been in years, but I still wasn't done yet. After gathering the sheet up, making sure all my hair was inside, I stuffed it back into the duffle bag before taking the bag and the clippers into the bathroom with me. Once I had my new pair of black jeans and matching t-shirt laid on the toilet, I put one of the hotel's complementary towels in the sink, took the clippers, and finished my transformation. When I was done grooming myself, I looked ten years younger. I made sure to put the towel in the bag with the sheet because both would burned later, and then I undressed for my shower. I was only under the hot water for a few seconds, when I heard the bathroom door open and just as quickly, Su'Ryah pulled the shower door open, wearing nothing except her beautiful smile.

"What are you doing, Su'ryah?"

"I'm showing you how much I missed you," she replied huskily, closing the distance between us and taking my dick in one hand, while her mouth found mine with fierce hunger. The time I'd been spending with Shawndra had taken my mind off of Su'Ryah, but I was quickly remembering how powerful our attraction was for one another. I'd had every intention of curving any advance she'd make towards me because my love for Shawndra was real and growing, but right now Su'Ryah had something else growing that I couldn't ignore. Before I could stop myself, I had her back against the shower wall, her legs wrapped around my waist, and my dick so far inside her that I could feel my balls slapping against her with every blow I delivered.

"D-De-Delontae! Delontae!" she moaned, holding on to me tight enough for me to feel her nails digging into my back.

Her pussy was tighter and wetter than I remembered, making it dangerous to fuck her at high speeds, but I kept pounding her the way I knew she needed. Within ten minutes, I felt her body spasm and buck against me right before her orgasm spun her eyes out of focus, and I still didn't slow down.

"I-I want it-I want it from th-the back," she stammered, breathlessly.

Without hesitation, I granted her wish, by dropping her to her feet, spinning her around, and diving right back inside her still throbbing pussy. I'd been in the world long enough to know you didn't touch a black woman's hair without permission, but I ignored that and grabbed a handful for leverage.

"Fuck me like you misssssed meeee!" she cried out, bracing herself against the wall before her head smashed into it.

Her demands tapped into a part of me that I'd been afraid to explore with Shawndra and before I knew it, I was fucking her with twenty years of rage driving me. When we finally climaxed, we both ended up on the shower floor with the water's spray pounding our limp bodies.

"I guess you did m-miss me," she said, chuckling.

"Maybe a little," I conceded, trying to catch my breath.

It took me a full five minutes to reel myself off the floor and help her up, so we could actually use the shower for what it was intended for.

"I can't believe I'm saying this, but you're actually sexier with your hair cut and your beard trimmed," she said, staring at me while I soaped my body and rinsed.

"Your opinion is biased, but thank you anyway."

"Biased or not, it's true. I know what you must've looked like in your younger years now, and you probably could've got the pussy then too!"

"Your ass is crazy, girl," I replied, shaking my head and smiling.

I could see the bad intentions clearly in her eyes, but I had work to do so I finished washing myself, and stepped out of the shower so she could do the same. Quickly getting dressed, I packed everything I intended to destroy in the duffle bag and went back into the room to make some necessary calls. Despite how much time I'd spent in prison, I still had reliable connections in the streets, so it didn't take long to run Keyshawn's credit report. He wasn't anybody special, but because his uncle made a name for himself during the height of the crack era, he wasn't exactly a nobody. Luckily for me, I didn't give a fuck *who* his uncle was, the boy and I had business.

"So, are you gonna tell me what your plan is now?" Su'Ryah asked, coming into the room beautifully naked and still dripping wet, towel in hand.

"You know I'm not gonna tell you, so why do you keep asking?"

"Because I love, because I want you to trust me enough to include me in all parts of your life, Delontae. Our patient/client relationship went way past compromised that first night you fucked me on my desk, and honestly I'm glad because I don't want a professional relationship with you. I want a *real* relationship with you, and we can't do that with secrets between us. I want you to trust me," she confessed, moving towards me until she was standing in front of me, looking me in my eyes. It was extremely hard to keep my focus on her face, with the scent of her gorgeous body invading my nostrils. I managed to keep steady eye contact as I searched my brain for the right words to use that wouldn't hurt her feelings.

"Su'Ryah, I *do* trust you and you know that, because despite how briefly we've known each other, you seem to get me in ways no one else has. With that being said, you know what I'm going to do. Whatever I *have* to do."

My statement didn't put fear in her eyes, nor did it seem to inspire judgment, and I'd kind of expected one of the two.

"I know you'll do what you have to do, and I accept that," she replied, convincingly.

"You accept that?"

"Yes, we may not be cut from the same cloth, but we come from the same trailer. I know you'll always protect yours no matter what happens, or what obstacles stand in your way, and I respect that. When you come back, I'll tell you why that exact quality means more to me every day I'm with you," she replied, giving me a quick kiss on the lips before going about the business of drying herself off.

Knowing her, that conversation would end with us trying to kill each other in the best possible way, but I'd worry about that when I returned.

"Are you gonna wait here, or are you leaving and coming back?" I asked.

"I'm not going anywhere, baby, I'll be waiting right here for you."

"Aight, I've got a stop to make so I'm gonna get on the road now," I said, gathering everything I needed and heading for the door.

"Delontae? Come back to me," she replied, vulnerably.

I winked at her before closing the door behind me, doing my best to leave all my emotions in that hotel room, because a distraction could get me killed. I'd just slid behind the wheel of my car when my phone started ringing. I pulled it out, thinking it would be Su'Ryah calling to finish her earlier declaration of love that she bit off, but instead I came face-to-face with Shawndra's number. With each ring, my guilt became more pronounced, until I felt like there was no room in the car to breathe around it. To ignore her would've been a bitch move though, and I wasn't no bitch.

"What's up?" I asked, finally answering her call.

"What do you mean, what's up? Why are you talking to me like some random female?" she asked, with obvious irritation.

"I'm sorry, babe, I'm just focused on what's going on down here. How are you?"

"Worried sick about you, asshole. Why didn't you at least call me when you got there?" she asked.

"I don't know. I guess I figured you wouldn't want to know what's going on down here, so I'd planned to call you when I had a handle on the situation."

"Delontae, I don't want details about whatever is going on, but of course I want to know if you and Maleah are okay. I love you both."

The truth in her declaration was soothing in a way I couldn't describe, but it also served in intensifying the guilt weighing on me about my situation with Su'ryah. It was crazy how I'd gone from not giving a fuck about nothing and no one, to caring for two women in a major way.

"I love you too, sweetheart, and I'm sorry for worrying you. Maleah is okay, she's out on bond, but she's under house arrest at her lawyer's house," I replied.

"She probably hates that, but it's better than sitting in a jail cell. Have you gotten to see her?"

"No, that's not a good decision, because she's most likely under surveillance. My focus is on fixing the situation so when she does go back to court, she walks out free and clear," I replied, determined.

When Shawndra fell silent, I knew it was because she was thinking about the things I'd most likely have to do to accomplish my goal, but that wasn't something I could apologize for. Her outlook on the usefulness of "The Lion" was one of the biggest things that separated her from Su'Ryah. I didn't necessarily like having to do the wrong thing for the right reason, but I understood that survival in life required compromise. Even moral compromise.

"I don't want you to lie to me, so I won't ask you how you plan to make that happen, I just want to know when you'll be coming back home?" she asked, softly.

"Soon, babe, I'll be back soon. Trust me when I tell you there's nowhere else in the world I'd rather be."

"Uh-huh, does your *doctor* know that?" she asked, sarcastically.

Her jealousy made me smile, but I knew now wasn't the time to encourage her games.

"You're cute, but I don't have time for this particular conversation. I'll call you back in a few hours, hopefully with good news."

"Okay, just be safe, please. James has a game tonight, so I'm gonna go and try to distract myself for a while. I love you, Delontae."

"I love you too, sweetheart, and make sure you tell the kids I love them," I replied, genuinely.

"I will, and good luck."

I hung up and started the car, once again working to center my focus on the task at hand as I got on the road. My theory about young Keyshawn having skeletons in his closet had proven true according to my sources, so my plan was simple. It was obvious he wasn't built to take his charge, because he would've done it already, which meant there was no need for me to sit down with him for some real nigga talk. He'd chosen his path, and that led me to mine. It took me two and a half hours to make it from the hotel in Maryland to the alley behind Lucy's Takeout, where I'd requested something be left for me. True enough, I already had a gun, but that one could one day be tracked back to Su'Ryah, which would either lead to me or put her in a fucked-up situation like this. It only took me a few minutes to find the brown paper bag hidden under the dumpster, and once I grabbed it, I was back in the car pulling off into the fading twilight.

From Lucy's, it was only a fifteen-minute drive over the bridge and into the neighborhood that Keyshawn worked, but

I took the scenic route to make sure I didn't pick up any unwanted guests. The extra ten minutes was worth the peace of mind. I parked four blocks away and waited until the night had swallowed me on all sides, before I pulled out the baby nine millimeter with the silencer. After checking it and rechecking it, I made sure to wipe it off, and put my gloves on before I tucked it into my hoodie pocket and got out of the car. I was from these streets, no matter how long I'd been gone, so I knew how to move without attracting the attention that an outsider would.

My plan was to go to the apartment Keyshawn trapped out of, put him down, and make it look like a robbery. As I neared the building though, I came face-to-face with the meaning behind the saying that if you wanted to hear God laugh, tell him what *you* had planned. The front stoop of the building was crowded, which was typical, but inconvenient as *fuck* right now. I counted four niggas standing around drinking, smoking, and talking shit, while another nigga was sitting on the steps getting his hair braided by some chick. I immediately recognized Keyshawn as the one getting his hair done from his most recent mug shot, which was good fortune on my part. The bad news for everybody else was that I didn't believe in leaving witnesses. I took a quick look around, followed by a deep breath, and then I pulled my gun out. They never saw it coming.

ARYANNA

Chapter 14

By the time I got back to my car, my heart rate had returned to normal, even though I could still taste the adrenaline on my tongue. It was funny to me how I could feel guilty about being dishonest with the women in my life, but I felt nothing close to that for the six lives I'd just snuffed out. In my mind, what I'd done was out of necessity, even though I knew it was wrong, but in my heart I felt...nothing. I got in the car, reloaded the gun in case I ran into any immediate static, and then pulled off into the night headed for my next destination. I made the drive to the chop shop I'd used when I was a teenager in Waldorf, Maryland, in just under two hours without any problems.

After collecting the twenty thousand dollars I'd agreed to for my Lexus, along with the keys to the seventy-eight black Mustang GT 5.0 that was included in the deal, I burned the duffle bag, dismantled the gun, and got back on the road. A short three hours after doing what some would consider unthinkable, I was pulling back into the DoubleTree parking lot, finally taking my first deep breath since I'd left Wisconsin. When I pulled out my phone to call Shawndra, I found a text message from her that immediately brought my anger back in full force. Apparently, I'd been right about her ex-husband not being smart enough to stay off my bad side, because he'd already fucked up by keeping the kids away from Shawndra. Her text message was telling me how he'd gone to her brother to search info on me, and of course my criminal background was laid out for his judgment. I shouldn't have been surprised, because my spiteful ex had contacted Shawndra's brother while I was still locked up, and told him all about me. That had led to her brother telling her parents, which had almost derailed our relationship, because the closest these white people came to the type of nigga I was, was the nightly news they watched.

People feared what they didn't understand, that was just a fact of life, and Shawndra's ex-husband was definitely one of those type of people. He should've been smart enough to know that I wasn't gonna let him use his kids against their mom though, I was *way* too much of a savage for that. I immediately tried calling her to let her know that, and to stop her from panicking, but she didn't answer. After five minutes of trying, I became frustrated enough to break my goddamn phone, but I figured she was probably still trying to resolve the situation on her own before I got involved. I put that problem to the back of my mind as I got out of the car and went into the hotel. When I got to Su'Ryah's room, I kicked myself for not getting the room key before I left, because now I would have to wake her up. I need not have worried though, because I didn't even make it through the first round of knocks before the door was opened and I was quickly pulled inside.

"Delontae, *tell me* you didn't do that!" Su'Ryah said, pushing up against the closed door.

"Do what? What the fuck are you talking about?" I asked, confused.

In response, she grabbed my hand and pulled me until I was standing next to her in front of the room's flat screen TV. When I looked at the screen, I understood her question because we were looking at CNN's coverage of a brutal, six-person homicide that happened in a low-income neighborhood in D.C. The shooting was being described as gruesome, due in part to some of the victims being shot in the face, and because the one girl in the bunch had only been sixteen years old. Police were saying that they thought the shootings were turf and drug related. My question was how the fuck had this made CNN because the last time I checked they didn't report hood politics.

"*This* has your name written all over it!" she said, angrily.

"How do you figure that?"

"Because I knew you were going to talk to him, Delontae! I know—"

"You're right. *You* know, and *you're* the only one who knows. So, what are you saying, Su'Ryah, I can't trust you?" I asked, carefully, looking at her closely.

"That's-that's not what I'm saying at all."

"What are you saying then, break it down for me so I have a clear understanding," I said, letting her hand go and taking a step away from her.

Even under the dim lighting of the TV, I could still see a sprinkle of fear dancing in her blue eyes, and despite my feelings for her I didn't say anything to elevate the fear. I was just hoping the gun concealed at the small of my back wouldn't be needed for this conversation.

"I'm simply saying you didn't have to do all of that Delontae, it was overkill, and anyone who truly knows you might become suspicious of you. Especially when the connection between Keyshawn and Maleah is discovered," she replied, calmer.

"First of all, I never said I *did* that, but even if I did it doesn't come back to me. The cops naturally assume I'm on the run somewhere *far* away from the District of Columbia, so I wouldn't be their first suspect, even with Keyshawn's connection to Maleah. Furthermore, the lifestyle that most of them niggas was living made them prime targets for an early death. Lastly, Keyshawn was still involved in that gun case, which will allow the conclusion to be drawn that he lived by the gun, so he died by it. Oh, and thanks to the magistrate judge, Maleah has an ironclad alibi. Did I miss anything?" I asked.

"She was sixteen, Delontae, just sixteen years old," Su'Ryah replied, clearly fighting all the emotions she was feeling. It was on the tip of my tongue to say I wouldn't choose anybody's daughter over my own, but I knew how cold that would come across. I wasn't trying to push my lack of morality in her face, because it could make her feel the need to stand on her own, if only to prove that she still had a soul.

"I didn't wish that on her, Su'Ryah. I think when it's all said and done, it'll come to light that she died from bullets that went through Keyshawn's head and into her abdomen. She wasn't a target, she was simply at the wrong place at the wrong time," I said, closing the distance between us and pulling her against me. The traces of fear I'd seen in her eyes were gone, but uncertainty had taken its place.

"You-you say that as if you know. What are you really saying?"

"I'm saying I'm sorry. You're better than this, better than *me,* and I'm sorry you're anywhere near life's ugliness," I replied, genuinely.

"I'm not better than you, Delontae, we come from the same mud remember? I just want better *for* you. You've lost so much of your life to the system already, and I don't want you to lose anymore."

"Don't worry, I won't," I replied, kissing her softly.

It wasn't my intent to open the flood gates of passion that existed between us, but the way she was clawing at my clothing told me I'd done just that.

130

"Babe, you know I have to go," I said, reluctantly pulling her hands away and kneeling in front of me. "Su'Ryah, I really need to get back because—"

My logical reasoning was lost when she wrapped her soft, succulent lips around the head of my dick and sucked all thought from my mind. As if that wasn't enough, she took both of my hands and put them on her head, and then opened her mouth wide to me while looking up at me with eyes full of submission. I pulled her towards me slowly at first, allowing her to adjust, but when I felt my dick banging at the back of her throat I gave in. Her skills were not to be denied, and even though she was letting me fuck her face, she kept just enough lip pressure around my dick to make me believe I was in her pussy. That resulted in me cumming hard in five minutes flat, and her swallowing every last drop.

"W-wow," I said, barely able to keep my balance as I watched her suck me completely limp.

"There's so much you have to learn about me," she replied, smiling and standing up.

"I see that, you could've gave a nigga a warning, though."

"Now, where's the fun in that? Besides, that was my way of accepting your apology and giving you one of my own. Before you left, I told you I accepted that you would do what you had to, but I turned around and jumped on you as soon as you got back. That wasn't right, and I'll work on not doing that again," she promised.

"Hopefully, there won't be any more situations that require you to feel like you're compromising who you are."

"I don't feel like my moral code is in question, because you and I live different lives. No matter what, I know you won't let me get too close to the stove to get burned," she replied.

"That's a fact. Speaking of which, I don't think it's a good idea for you to be around Maleah just yet. Don't get me wrong, I want you to keep a close eye on her so she stays out of shit, but you lead directly back to me and we don't need that right now."

"I understand. I'll communicate through my cousin until you tell me otherwise. Is there anything you need me to tell her?"

"If she's a competent lawyer, she'll be able to spin Keyshawn's death and get Maleah off without a problem," I replied, giving her a look that made it clear. Anything other than that outcome would be unacceptable.

"She'll take care of it, Delontae, and when it's all over, I'll move Maleah in with me."

"You-you don't have to do that," I replied, surprised by her offer.

"I know I don't *have* to, I *want* to. I'm in no way trying to replace her mom, but it's obvious that she needs someone right now, and her family either can't or won't be there for her. You've proven how much your daughter means to you, and even though I'm grateful for every moment we get to spend together, I don't want a reoccurrence of tonight's events. I'll take care of Maleah, I promise."

I didn't know what to say. Doctor Su'Ryah Davenport was a woman of many surprises, and she just kept hitting me with them, which only made my feelings for her more intense. I knew how I felt about Shawndra, but was it possible that I was falling for this beautiful woman in front of me too? That question was too deep for a quick analysis, so I tucked it away for a later date.

"Thank you," I replied, giving her a quick kiss, before zipping my pants up and going to the mini bar.

132

"You don't have to thank me, it'll be good practice anyway."

I was deep off in the bar looking for a soda, so it took a few moments for her last statement to register to me.

"'Practice,' what's that mean?" I asked slowly, studying her.

"That means one day I plan to be a mom, so spending time with Maleah will help me have my maternal instincts."

I *believed* what she was saying, but I felt like there was *more* to what she was saying. I let it go though, grabbed my Sprite, and prepared to make my exit. I wasn't looking forward to making this long-ass drive tonight, but I needed to put space between me and what I'd done ASAP.

'How long do you plan on staying here?" I asked.

"Just 'til check-out time in the morning. You sure you're okay to drive wherever it is you're going?"

"I'll be fine," I replied, pulling ten thousand dollars out of my pocket and passing it to her.

"You can keep the extra for any expenses that come with Maleah, and I'll send you more once I get some things situated."

"I can't take all of this money, Delontae, you'll need some and—"

"I'm good, don't worry. If I need something, I'm not too proud to ask my woman," I replied.

The way she smiled at me told me she thought I was referring to her with the "my woman" comment, but I actually hadn't been. I was smart enough not to say that though.

"I like a man who knows pride can be overrated, and luckily for you, I'm a woman who enjoys taking care of her man."

"I thought a man was a complication in your life that you didn't need or want," I replied, tossing her words from a previous conversation back at her.

"I think I've proven that you're a complication I can handle, and *definitely* one I want," she said, seductively, moving towards me with those same bad intentions in her eyes.

"Don't start nothing, the last thing we need is for me to be balls' deep in you and I get caught up by the law. I'm careful, but I'm not perfect."

"I understand, baby. Besides, it'll just make the next time even better. In case you're unclear on when that'll be, my vacation time is in six weeks and I've already notified all of my patients, so there won't be anything holding me back. Where shall we rendezvous?" she asked, expectantly.

"Nice try, but I'll let you know," I replied, pulling her towards me for one last kiss before turning for the door.

"Be safe, Delontae, and call me when you get where you're going."

I promised I would before disappearing from her view and making my way back to my car. The Mustang might've been a downgrade from the Lexus coupe, but I felt more comfortable in this car because it wouldn't draw attention. After a quick stop at 7-Eleven for a giant cup of strong black coffee, I got on the highway and once again attempted to outrun my past. I wanted to call Shawndra and tell her that I was coming home, but with the late hour, I decided to let her sleep and simply surprise her.

By ten a.m., I was pulling up in front of her house, completely exhausted and yearning for any bed that would have me. Before I'd gotten out of my car, I'd seen Shawndra's SUV in her driveway, but I hadn't paid any attention to the navy blue Cadillac Escalade parked beside her, until I was right up on it. I didn't know who it belonged to, which made me hesitate on my approach, but I was honestly too tired to get back in my car and go anywhere else. At this moment, I was thankful my appearance didn't scream "fresh out of prison", just in case it was her parents inside. I went to the front door with the intention of knocking, but I could immediately feel the bass from the loud rap music being played inside. That told me it *definitely* wasn't her parents inside which made me relax a little, but now my curiosity was piqued. I tried the door knob and was surprised to feel it turn with ease beneath my grip as the door opened. I'd never been in Shawndra's house, but I immediately took the stairs down into what I assumed was the basement, because that's where the music was coming from. What I saw when I got down there, turned my blood to ice and before I knew it, I could feel the weight of my pistol in my hand. I didn't know what was fucking with me more, the fact that Shawndra was laid out on her couch asshole naked and obviously high, or that the nigga sitting next to her was bagging up dope. Knowing her past, it was a safe bet that dude was dealing meth. My approach was quiet and unnoticed, until I turned off the music.

"No fast moves, my nigga, just keep bagging up your product," I said, calmly.

"Who, who the fuck are you?" he asked, looking from Shawndra to me, and back to her.

She was looking right at me, but it took a long moment for recognition to catch up with her voice box.

"Delontae, you're back," she said slowly, waving sloppily at me.

She was *definitely* high, but I knew how to fix that.

"Who's your friend, Shawndra?" I asked, closing the distance between us until I was standing between her and him.

"Ah, man, I just—"

I cut his sentence short by smacking him ruthlessly in the mouth with the butt of my gun, adding blood and teeth to his pile of dope on the table.

"Wasn't talking to you, bruh, so I advise you to keep your mouth shut. Answer my question, Shawndra," I demanded, in the same calm tone.

"Not-not a friend, just my ex. Needed him because William took the kids away," she replied, fighting mightily against the unconsciousness that comes with nodding out on Meth.

I knew from the many conversations we'd had about this old, beat-down nigga, that he'd been her supplier of the horse galloping through her veins right now, and they'd fucked occasionally. He may have been fully clothed at the moment, but he'd *absolutely* fucked up as far as I was concerned. I grabbed her by a fistful of her hair and pulled her into an upright position, making sure our faces were only inches apart.

"Can you hear me, baby? Need you to pay attention to what I'm about to tell you, because it's important," I said, with a normal tone.

"Aww! Delontae, my hair, you're hurting me," she whined, trying to loosen the grip I had on her.

"Bitch, *listen* to me," I growled through gritted teeth, as pure rage flooded my veins.

"I'm listening!" she cried.

For a moment, I could see through all the drugs in her system. I could see the pain, the shame, and the anger that she'd obviously been trying to erase with her self-destructive actions and seeing that told me that there was hope for her.

"Look at him," I said, turning her head until she was eye to eye with her pusher man.

"Look at the nigga who was so quick to tear you down and exploit your pain for his own benefit. Look at the worthless motherfucker you were willing to sacrifice *our* family for, and *our* kids for. Look at him!" I screamed in her ear.

"Delontae, please, I get it. I—"

"No, you don't get it because if you did, you never would've put yourself in this fucking position! Maybe this will help you to truly understand," I said, pressing the barrel of my gun to his forehead.

"Delontae, I *get it*, I swear. I—"

"You still looking at him?" I asked.

"Yes, I am, but—"

The roar of the bullet tearing through her ex's brain shut her up, and his brain fragments splattering on her made her vomit violently on his corpse.

"Remember what just happened the next time you think about fucking relapsing. Now, get yourself cleaned up, because you're going to an NA meeting."

ARYANNA

Chapter 15

I had better control of my anger forty-five minutes later when Shawndra emerged from her bedroom, looking a lot less high, but I could still feel the thirst for blood threatening to overtake me. The thoughts of what she might have been doing with this nigga all night were enough to make me homicidal, but knowing that she'd allowed her weak-ass ex-husband to push her into relapse had the lion ready to roar. On top of all that fury was also my disappointment in Shawndra, and I knew I'd have to deal with that first, whether I wanted to or not.

"Delontae, we didn't have sex," she said, immediately crossing the room to stand next to me, in a way that prevented her from having to look at the dead body slumped next to me on the couch. I didn't respond to her statement, but instead continued bagging up the remainder of the dead man's dope.

"I *swear* we didn't have sex," she repeated, insistently.

"Really? From the looks of things, he definitely fucked you," I replied, still not bothering to look up from the task at hand.

"I fucked up and I know that, but we *did not* have sex, please believe me."

"Do you think that's all I give a fuck about? Are you that stupid?" I asked, coldly.

I knew calling her stupid would hurt her feelings because other men had done nothing except put her down in the past, but it would also let her know how truly pissed I was.

"Delontae, please don't talk to me like that because it makes me feel like you've given up on me, and on us," she replied, tearfully.

"Shouldn't I give up? It's obvious this dope is worth more to you than whatever I could offer."

"No, it's *not*! I had a moment of weakness and I made a mistake. I'm not *perfect,* Delontae, no one is. And the reality of losing my kids put me in a dark place," she replied, her voice laced with anger and pain.

When I looked up at her, I saw the fight in her eyes that I remembered from our days of visitation, when I was locked up. She wasn't no weak bitch, but I had to make sure she understood that, or *mistakes* would continue to happen.

"The reality of losing your kids? Why would that be a reality and not a temporary thing? Have you really *not* realized who I am, and that these are *our* kids? I ain't *never* let a motherfucker take nothing from me, and your bitch-ass baby daddy ain't about to be the first. There are rules to this though, and rule number one is that I can't fight for no one who won't fight themselves. So, what are you gonna do?" I asked, pushing a stamp bag of dope in her direction. We both knew I'd just issued her a two-part test, but one decision was more difficult than the other.

"He's their dad, Delontae, if you kill him it'll affect them too."

"I know that, and that's the only reason I'm gonna let him live. I'm just gonna have a talk with him, as soon as you give me his address," I replied.

She hadn't looked at the dope on the table or made a move towards what I'd tried to give her, which led me to believe she was sure about her decision to leave it alone. The look she was giving me told me she was *unsure* about my ability to simply talk to William.

"You won't kill him, you promise?" she asked, skeptically.

"I'll let him live *this* time, but if her crosses me wrong again, we'll have to revisit this topic of conversation."

"He lives in Fitchburg, I'll text you the address," she replied, heading back to her room and returning with her phone.

While she was doing that, I did a quick count of all the stamp bags of meth. I pressed by the almost five hundred total count.

"Ay man, I appreciate the work, bruh. I'll just hold your cut of the money I'ma make until you come back to get it," I said, looking at the dead man next to me and laughing softly.

"That's, that's sick, why are you talking to a dead body?" she asked, clearly horrified.

"Just trying to lift his spirits and loosen him up. He's a little stiff."

"You're *not* funny! What are you gonna do about him anyway?" she asked, doing everything she could to avoid looking at him.

"You mean what are *we* gonna do, right? This nigga wouldn't be here if it wasn't for you."

"I-I don't know what to do, you're 'The Lion,'" she replied, using her fingers to make air quotes.

"Thought there was no place for 'The Lion' in Madison, Wisconsin?"

She opened her mouth to speak, but quickly realized that she was a victim of her own words and closed her mouth. The fish-like motion made me smile.

"I need you to go to a hardware store and buy a chainsaw," I said.

"Why?" she asked, slowly.

"Because I'm not about to try and carry anything that looks like a body out of this house. I need you to get heavy duty trash bags too, and do you have any bleach?"

"Yeah, in the laundry room. I'll get it," she replied, spinning on her heels and quickly leaving the room.

I didn't know where the laundry room was, but I could hear her vomiting again, which told me she'd made a necessary detour. I wasn't surprised. I'd always known that she wasn't built for this type of action. What did surprise me was the fact that I hadn't questioned whether or not I needed to kill her to make sure my latest indiscretion stayed a secret. I'd literally just blown a man's head off, and *made* her watch while I did it, but not once did I ask myself if she'd turn my black ass in. To say that wasn't normal of me was an understatement, because there was no statute of limitations on murder, and hell hath no fury like a woman scorned. The only conclusion I could draw from my actions was that I actually trusted her. I let that thought simmer in my mind while watching her come back towards me with a bottle of Clorox in her hand.

"It's brand-new," she said, passing it to me.

I could see clearly the drugs were almost completely out of her system, which meant the real work could begin.

"What time is the meeting?" I asked.

"There's one in thirty minutes, but—"

"No buts, you're going, Shawndra."

"I know, jeez, just listen to me for a minute. A lot of times, people who go to the NA meetings do it because it's court-ordered, but they're still getting high. I can move some of this stuff for you," she offered.

I had to take a deep breath, so I wouldn't laugh in her face, especially since I knew she was serious.

"You want me to give you meth to sell? Seriously?"

"You want to try selling it yourself? I can't stop you, but you're not from around here so you'll stick out to the cops, and we know how much you need *that* right now," she replied, sarcastically.

I didn't like her idea, but I couldn't fault her logic, any more than I could ignore how much I *really* didn't need any type of police action in my life. The real problem was that I didn't need her getting caught up or being tempted to fuck up.

"I understand your logic, but I still don't think it's a good idea," I replied, honestly.

"If you're thinking I'll get high, trust me. I won't," she said, looking at the dead body still occupying her couch.

"This is a lot of dope to move, and if you get caught up, you'll be looking at serious time. We both know you ain't built for that, sweetheart."

"You're right. I'm not, but I know you'd never let me go to prison, so I'm not worried about that part. I won't try to move all of it at once, I'll spread it out, even if I have to pick up a few more meetings," she replied, confidently.

Her faith in me stroked my ego, but I couldn't let that be the deciding factor. Ultimately, I was gonna do it because I believed in her, despite how I'd found her when I got here, and I felt like she was trying to prove something to me. I counted out twenty bags, bundled them, and tossed them to her.

"Will that be enough?" I asked.

"Should be. I'm gonna leave them here though while I run and get what you need, so you can handle that situation as quick as possible."

"That's fine," I replied, standing up and undressing so I could move the body to the bathroom for dismantling.

Suddenly time wasn't of the essence, because Shawndra stood there watching me strip until I was wearing absolutely nothing.

ARYANNA

"You're not getting any of this," I said, holding my dick so she knew exactly what I was talking about.

"What? Why? I told you we did *not* have sex."

"That still don't mean you're off the hook. Now, go handle your business," I replied, preparing to get to work myself.

I could hear her mumbling under her breath, but she did it as she was walking away. After I moved the body from the couch to the bathtub, I got to work erasing all evidence of the dopeman's life and death as it pertained to this house. Before I knew it, Shawndra had returned with what I needed, and promised to be back to help with the clean-up when the meeting was over. As soon as she left, I took the saw and broke my man down into big barbecue pieces, filling up three trash bags with him. I'd just finished cleaning up the bloody mess I'd made in the bathroom when Shawndra returned again. This time, dragging a machine in tow.

"What the hell is that?" I asked.

"It's a Rug Doctor, but I can use it to clean carpets and furniture. I figured we'd need it."

"Good thinking. You get started on that while I take a shower, and stop looking at me like that, because you're not taking a shower with me," I stated, closing the bathroom door.

In my mind, I knew I really didn't have a leg to stand on, but the fact that some nigga had even *seen* Shawndra naked made me want to kill him again! I was being irrational, considering what I'd done with Su'ryah, but lack of sleep had me not caring about whether I was being irrational or not. I took a quick ten-minute shower, and then went back into the living room to get dressed in front of her out of spite. It didn't have the desired affect though, because she was focused on her cleaning.

144

"I'll take care of the trash bags when I get back," I said, gathering up all the dope and extra baggies off the table.

"Wait, where are you going?"

"To talk to William real quick. I'll be back," I replied, stuffing everything into the huge Ziploc bag the recently deceased had been using.

"Delontae, when was the last time you slept? You can't go out like that. Your brain is not functioning at full speed right now. Take a nap first."

"A nap? Do I look like a toddler to you? I'm going—"

"You're gonna take your ass in that room and go to fucking sleep, because you know that's exactly what you should do," she said, pushing me in the direction of her bedroom.

If I thought she was bullshitting, the fact that she pushed me in the room and closed the door made it clear how serious she was. Suddenly, looking at her bed made my eyelids heavy and forced me to admit a nap was needed. As soon as my head hit the pillow, the whole world went dark, and I didn't have another conscious thought until I felt like I was having the best wet dream ever. I awoke to find Shawndra on top of me, completely naked and beautiful in the moon's light, riding my dick slow and steady. The look in her eyes was love and pain, and both were seeking my forgiveness. Without breaking stride, she took my hands and put them on her breasts, making it impossible for me not to squeeze them and play with her nipples the way she liked. With each twist and pinch of her taut flesh, I could feel her pussy thumping harder and getting wetter. Suddenly, she kicked her legs out straight behind her and brought us body to body, kissing me passionately as she continued riding me slowly. My hands found their way to her juicy ass cheeks and we worked together to chase complete fulfillment.

"In-in love with you," she paused, into my mouth.

"In love with you too, baby," I replied, lifting into her downward motion faster and harder.

Within minutes, we came together, swallowing each other's screams of ecstasy. I wanted to go back to sleep just like we were, but a quick look at the clock told me it was three a.m., which made it a good time to handle business.

"I want you to come with me," I said, wrapping my arms around her so she couldn't move.

"I did cum with you, didn't you feel it?" she asked, teasingly.

"I'm serious, babe. I need to get rid of your friend and his truck, so I need you to take me somewhere I can burn everything. You can drive my car, and then we'll go visit William."

"Where *is* your car? I didn't see it when I went out earlier?" she asked.

"I got rid of the Lexus. The Mustang out front is mine now, but I'll let you drive it this one time."

"Gee, thanks. I guess I'll go with you then, but I don't think it's a good idea for me to go inside the house," she replied.

"We're in agreement about that, but let me play devil's advocate for a second. If the kids wake up, wouldn't it be better for you to be inside to distract?"

My question was one that provoked thought and had her silent for a moment, but she eventually shook her head in agreement.

"You're right, I don't want the kids to see or hear anything, but now that I'm thinking about it, I don't think you should go in the house at all. William should be leaving for work in a couple hours, so if we take care of the problem first, we should run into him outside," she replied, thoughtfully.

"I think I'm starting to rub off on you because you're thinking more and more like a criminal."

"Oh God, I hope not," she said, laughing as she climbed off of me.

Now that we had a working plan of action, we both dressed quickly. And once I had the trash bags loaded into the Escalade we got on the road, with her leading the way. I didn't like having to dispose of a body in unfamiliar territory, but Shawndra assured me that she knew Cross Plains well, because she'd grown up there. After an hour of zigzagging, she led me down a dead-end street. I doused the inside of the SUV with the lighter fluid and gasoline we'd brought, lit the blaze, and we disappeared into the night on to our next destination.

"I think you should let me handle this situation with William," she said, suddenly.

"I think if you could've dealt with this situation, I wouldn't have just had to dispose of a body."

"Not like it's the first time," she mumbled, under her breath.

"Yeah whatever, that still doesn't change the fact that you just gave up your years of sobriety, and now you want me to believe you can handle this?"

"So does this mean you're gonna try to *handle* difficult situations for me for the rest of my life, like I can't take care of my fucking self?" she asked, angrily.

"*Can* you take care of yourself?" I replied, crudely. When she turned to look at me, I could see I'd hurt her feelings, just like I could see the guilt she was battling over her most recent decisions. We rode the rest of the way in silence, pulling up in front of her ex's house at a quarter to five in the morning.

"By the way, here's your money," she said, pulling a wad of bills from her pocket and tossing it in my lap. I did a quick count of the two hundred dollars before tossing it back to her.

"You keep it."

"Nope, I don't want you feeling like you have to take care of me," she replied, tossing the money back at me.

"I don't *have* to take care of you, I *want* to," I said, taking her hand in my own in hopes of ending the fight we were having.

Her squeezing my hand in response told me at the very least, we were gonna table this disagreement for now. That turned out to be a smart decision on both of our parts because sooner than expected, William appeared out of the pre-dawn gloom. I could tell he was moving without a care in the world, not unlike most law-abiding free white men. The only difference between him and the average motherfucker was that he now had me for an enemy.

"Be ready to go, but don't start the car until you see me walking back towards you," I said, pulling out my pistol as I quickly slipped from the car.

My moves towards William were swift and stealthy, bringing me face-to-face with him before he knew what was happening.

"Morning little Willie," I said, smiling at the look of utter terror that came over his face.

"Wh-what do you want?"

"Just to talk. I heard you've been doing a lot of talking *about* me, so I figured you'd want to talk *to* me."

"N-no-no, I don't. There's n-nothing I want to say to you," he stammered nervously, looking around with obvious desperation.

"You sure? Well, that's okay, because I've got a couple things that I want to run past you, so—"

"I've gotta go-go to work," he said, quickly reaching for the door to his truck.

Before he could get the door opened, I jammed the barrel of my gun into his right eye socket.

"It's rude to interrupt me when I'm trying to have a peaceful conversation with you, little Willie. Would you prefer we had this conversation inside, where I'm sure your wife is still sleeping?" I asked, calmly.

"N-no."

"Didn't think so, I'll make this quick, simple, and painless for you. Don't *fuck* with Shawndra again. Don't use the kids against her or even *think* about keeping them away from her. I know you asked about me, but to be honest with you, Shawndra's brother only knows a *fraction* of the shit I've really done in my life. I want you to understand that if you cross me or Shawndra again, you'll be the *last* person I kill, because I'll kill everyone you care about first. Except for the kids, of course. Do you understand, little Willie?" I asked, stepping closer to him so he could look in my eyes and know I wasn't bluffing.

"I understand, please don't sh-shoot me," William begged, with tears in his eyes.

"I'll let you live, this time."

ARYANNA

Chapter 16

One month later

"Yo, Dad, guess what?" Maleah said, with a grin on her face wide enough to take up my whole screen on my phone.

"What?"

"The charges got dropped!" she replied, excitedly.

I knew my smile was now matching hers as I breathed a much needed sigh of relief. Su'Ryah hadn't told me why she'd wanted me to call, only that it was important, and I was glad she had insisted.

"That's good shit, sweetheart, now please don't put yourself in another situation like that."

"I won't, Dad. After what happened to Keyshawn I realized I could've easily been that young girl who caught that stray bullet just for being around the wrong nigga. That's not how I want my life to end," she replied, shaking her head.

There was no way I could ever tell Maleah I was the one responsible for killing those people that night, nor could I be proud of what I'd done. I was glad my daughter had taken something positive away from the situation, though.

"That's good to hear because you know I be worried about you," I confessed.

"Yeah, I know. But I'm good, Daddy, thanks to you and Su'Ryah."

When she'd mentioned Su'Ryah's name, she turned the phone her way so I could see her, and the smile she gave me made my heartbeat faster. Luckily, Shawndra was in the bedroom and I was in the living room, or an explanation would've been required.

"So, what's next?" I asked, focusing back on Maleah.

"Well, I've been saving all the money I can from what you've been sending, plus Su'Ryah helped me get a part-time job. College is still my ultimate goal. I'm just waiting on my PSAT scores so I can narrow down my choices of schools."

"Tell him the rest," Su'Ryah urged, gently.

I noticed the look they exchanged, but I held my tongue and waited for Maleah to speak.

"I uh, was thinking about going to either Howard or Georgetown University."

"Two good schools that would be lucky to have you, but you *do* realize that you'd still be in D.C. right?" I asked.

"Duh, Dad."

"I'm just making sure because the last time we discussed furthering your education, you told me you wanted to go *far* away," I said.

"You'd be surprised how far away I feel from my old life just being here with Su'Ryah. She's offered to let me stay with her as long as I want."

I could tell without asking that Maleah liked that idea, and she was happier than I'd seen her since I'd come home. I was in no position to disrupt her life once again, but it would've been irresponsible of me not to make certain that Su'Ryah wasn't being imposed upon.

"Give the phone to Su'Ryah and let us talk for a minute," I requested.

"Okay. I love you, and you *better* call me back," she demanded, before passing the phone.

"Love you too," I replied, laughing.

"About time you tell me how you really feel," Su'ryah said, smiling, as Maleah left the room.

"What's understood doesn't need to be said, Doc. How are you holding up out there?"

"I'm good, I miss you though. I'm sooo looking forward to my vacation time," she replied, smiling seductively.

"Yeah, uh, about that do you think it's a good idea to link up? I mean you could still be under surveillance."

"I'm not stupid, Delontae, and you know I'll be careful. It almost sounds like you don't want to see me."

"You know that's not it at all, babe, I just don't want you caught up in no bullshit. It's clear Maleah has come to depend on you a lot," I replied, smoothly.

"She has, and my love grows for her every day. Just like my love for you. I need to see you, Delontae. I need to spend time with you, even if it's only to have a face-to-face conversation. FaceTime is so impersonal when it's the only way we communicate in our relationship."

"I understand what you're saying, so let me know exactly when you're on vacation. In the meantime, let's talk about my baby," I said, seeing Shawndra's bedroom door open and her appear.

I thought she was about to come in my direction, but she went upstairs without looking at me, making me wonder if she'd heard my conversation despite me turning the volume on my phone down.

"What about our baby?" Su'Ryah asked, snapping my attention back to her. The question she asked didn't catch me off guard, the fact that she referred to Maleah as *our* baby did though. I chose to let it slide and push on.

"Is her staying there really what you want? I know you care about her, but making you an instant mom ain't fair to you."

"Delontae, I fully understood what I was taking on when you were here and we had our conversation about this, and

153

nothing has changed. You're worried about the wrong thing," she replied, winking at me.

A smartass remark was on the tip of my tongue, but seeing Shawndra headed my way put the brakes on that shit *quick*. The look on her face told me that she had something on her mind, and the fact that she was approaching me with her hands behind her back had me a little nervous.

"What's wrong?" I asked.

"Nothing, absolutely nothing," Shawndra replied, smiling like she was the owner of a juicy secret.

"Delontae, who are you talking to?" Su'Ryah asked.

I opened my mouth to tell her I'd call her back, but the pregnancy test Shawndra was handing me froze my facial expression.

"I wish you could see your face right now," Shawndra said, laughing.

"Is-is this real?" I asked, taking it and reading the word "pregnant" in the little window.

"Yep," Shawndra yelled, excitedly.

"Is what real? Delontae, what the fuck is going on?" Su'Ryah asked, clearly frustrated.

"I'ma, uh, call you back," I replied, hanging up and turning my phone off so Shawndra had my undivided attention.

"You're pregnant?"

"No, *we're* pregnant. At least, I *thought* we were in this together, but you—"

"I didn't let her thoughts of doubt leave her mouth before I jumped up and pulled her into my arms, kissing her passionately. By the time I finally released her, she was fighting to catch her breath.

"Still think we're not in this together?" I asked, smiling at her.

"Huh?" she replied, clearly flustered.

I could only laugh at her facial expression, and then I kissed her senseless again.

"B-babe, if you don't stop we're gonna be late," she said, pulling back so she could look up at me.

"Late? Late for what?'

"Well, I figured as soon as I told you the news, you'd be beating me in the head to go see a doctor, so I scheduled my appointment already. We've got thirty minutes to get there," she replied.

"I love that you know me," I confessed, kissing her again.

"I do know you, and I know if you don't stop kissing me, we're gonna end up in the bedroom trying for twins," she replied, laughing and backing reluctantly out of my arms, I couldn't deny the truth she spoke, so I didn't try. Instead, I put my phone in my pocket, grabbed my car keys and followed her lead out of the house.

"Uh, where are you going?" I asked, watching her go for the driver's side of my car.

"I think I've earned the right to drive your baby since I'm giving you an *actual* baby," she replied, holding her hand out for the keys.

I gave them to her without argument, and climbed my happy ass into the passenger seat. As we pulled off, my mind went back to all the plans we'd made and conversations we'd had while I was locked up I about this exact thing. We'd dreamed of one day having a baby together, knowing we were racing against a clock, because neither of us was getting any younger. It was something we'd both wanted so badly that it had been difficult to speak the words sometimes, because with hope we always had to acknowledge the devastation on the opposite side of that coin. The last month we'd spent together had felt less and less like playing house, and more like laying the foundation upon which the dreams we'd spoken of could be built. Despite coming from completely different walks of life we seemed to fit together like peanut butter and jelly, and I know that having a baby would only strengthen that bond.

"I love you," I declared, taking her free hand in mine and kissing it.

"I love you too. I know I interrupted your call, but was everything okay in D.C.?"

"More than okay. Maleah beat the gun charge," I replied, smiling as I thought about the future that lay in front of my children.

Shawndra never asked me what I'd done when I'd made the trip back to D.C., and we never spoke about the night of her relapse. We'd both made decisions we weren't proud of, but we chose to focus on building a life together, instead of judging each other.

"That's great, babe, so now what's she gonna do?" Shawndra asked.

"She still focused on going to college, but I think she's gonna stay in that area because she likes living with Su'Ryah."

"And Doctor Davenport is okay with that?" she asked.

It didn't escape me that Shawndra had gone formal when discussing Su'Ryah, or that the temperature of her voice had gotten chillier all of a sudden. I wasn't gonna feed into it though.

"Yeah, she actually wants Maleah to stay around, that's what we were talking about when you gave me the best news *ever*," I replied, kissing her hand again and smiling hard enough to make my checks hurt.

"You should call them back and tell them the good news."

To anybody else, her suggestion would've sounded innocent, nothing more than an expectant mother sharing the good news. I knew better though, because Shawndra was the queen of petty, and had absolutely no problem throwing shade at a bitch.

"That's something I can worry about later. Right now, I just want to focus on you and our baby. How far along do you think you are?" I asked, steering the conversation in the right direction.

"Only a few weeks. And before you say anything stupid, I *did not* have sex that night and I'll gladly give you a DNA test if you want."

"Baby, stop being defensive because the thoughts you're thinking never crossed my mind. I know whose baby you're carrying," I replied, confidently.

We'd just pulled up to a stop light, which allowed her the opportunity to look me in the eyes and study my face for doubt, but I knew she would find none. I trusted her unequivocally, not just with the secrets of the deaths I'd delivered, but now with the new life she was nurturing. She leaned in and gave me a quick kiss, before continuing our drive. Fifteen minutes later, we arrived at her doctor's office, and only had to wait a short ten minutes to be seen. Knowing me as well as she did, Shawndra had scheduled herself for a full medical work-up, including blood work, and STD tests. I could only smile in appreciation for her attention to detail, and her obvious respect for the tendency I had to micromanage everything. An hour and a half later, we left the doctor's office with the news she was four weeks pregnant, a clean bill of health, and with a list of acceptable foods Shawndra could eat to keep her diabetes under control.

"Baby, will you be nice and let me have what I'm craving when it gets really bad?" she asked, once we were back in the car.

"I don't know, it depends."

"On?" she persisted.

"On what you're willing to *do* to get what you want," I replied, teasingly.

"Oh, Lord," she said, rolling her eyes and laughing, as she started the car and pulled out of the parking lot.

"Where are we going?"

"Just because I sold all of the meth doesn't mean I don't need to go to any more meetings. Besides, now I can go back to the Monona Serenity group," she replied.

I admired her determination, and I knew she hadn't really felt comfortable going to random meetings and sharing. It would be good for her to be with the group she felt safe owning her truth around.

"Okay, well do you want me to drop you off and come back, or do you wanna take me to the house?" I asked.

"Actually, I wanna do something we talked about a while ago—"

"Sex in public!" I blurted, smiling wickedly.

"*No*! I want you to come to the meeting with me, you know, for support. You could use it too."

"I understand you wanting me to support you, but what do you mean, 'I could use it too?'" I asked, looking at her curiously.

"Come on, babe, you've gotta admit that you battle addiction too."

"You're fucking with me right now, right? I don't get high and you *know* it," I replied, laughing her suggestion off.

"You don't get high off of drugs, no. You get high off of *violence*, that's what you're addicted to."

Her statement froze the smile on my face and forced the laugh to die in my throat. I loved her too much to argue with the truth, even if I didn't like it, so I kept my mouth shut while giving her statement considerable thought.

"Touché," I replied, softly.

"Baby, I didn't say that to hurt you. You should know by now that I love you regardless," she professed, sincerely.

"I know you do, and I'm man enough to admit you might have a point. So, we'll do this together."

Seeing her smile was enough to make me know that I was doing the right thing, even if it was uncomfortable for me. There was nothing I wouldn't do for this woman. We arrived at the Monona Serenity group five minutes before the meeting was set to start, but there were still people getting their last cigarettes in, so there was no rush. As soon as we parked, I could feel Shawndra's tension radiating from her, and I knew she was remembering her last experience in this particular parking lot.

"It's okay, babe, I'm with you," I said, taking her hand in mine and squeezing it reassuringly.

When she looked at me I could tell she'd gathered the needed strength, and once she squeezed my hand in return we got out of the car.

"Hey Shawndra, long time no see," a short redhead said, when we'd made it to the sidewalk in front of the building.

"Yeah I know, I've had a lot going on," Shawndra replied, taking my hand possessively.

"Who's your friend? I haven't seen him before," the redhead commented.

"I have. Only once though, on the night my brother was found dead."

ARYANNA

Chapter 17

I made sure to keep my expression completely blank as my gaze swung to the slender brunette who'd joined the redhead. The look in her face wasn't exactly accusatory, but it wasn't friendly either. Once thing I knew for sure was that I'd never seen this chick before now, but if she was the sister of the man who'd tried to rape my woman, this could get ugly.

"What are you talking about, Stacy, John is dead?" Shawndra asked, pulling off a believable shocked expression.

"Yeah, a little more than a month ago someone found him with his neck broken on the side of the building," Stacy replied, still looking at me.

"I'm sorry for your loss," I said.

"Thank you. I did see you here that night, right? You were pulling in as I was leaving," Stacy replied, making it clear to everyone listening that she was making a positive identification.

"Babe, that was the night you surprised me when you came into town unexpected," Shawndra stated, looking at me.

I knew she meant well, but she was making the classic mistake of volunteering too much information.

"Where are you from? The redhead asked, curiously.

"L.A., born and raised," I lied smoothly, smiling.

"I didn't catch your name," Stacy commented, casually.

We both knew I hadn't given my name, but her statement let me know that she was with the bullshit.

"I'm sorry, Stacy, I was so shocked hearing about John that I forgot my manners. Angela, Stacy, this is my boyfriend, Derrick," Shawndra said, smiling up at me. I

161

could feel the sea of questions getting ready to pour from these women's mouths, but the sight of everyone moving into the building meant the meeting was starting, and the interrogation would have to wait.

"Nice to meet you," Angela said, extending her hand to me.

I shook it, expecting for Stacy to do the same, but she'd already turned on her heels and was headed inside.

"We'll see you in there, Ang, I'm just gonna have a quick smoke," Shawndra said, pulling out her cigarettes.

I waited until Angela was out of sight before I smacked the pack of cigarettes out of her hand.

"Hey!" she exclaimed, looking at me like I'd lost my damn mind.

"You're pregnant, you can't smoke."

"I knew that," she mumbled, sheepishly.

"You didn't tell me dude had a sister."

"I didn't see how it was important, and I've put everything about him and that night out of my mind," she replied.

Even though the act of rape hadn't been committed, I could still understand her being traumatized by the attack and wanting to forget it. The problem was that dude's sister wasn't likely to forget her brother's death, and she'd made it clear that I was on her radar. That could turn out bad, and I had too much to lose.

"I think Stacy is gonna be a problem," I said, thoughtfully.

"What do you mean?"

The look I leveled at her said that she knew *exactly* what I meant.

"*No,* Delontae, come on now. You can't just go around killing people," she replied, in a forced whisper.

"I didn't *say* I was gonna kill her, I—"

"You didn't *have* to say it, Delontae. I know how you think, and if you think she's a problem there's only *one* way you know how to solve it. You can't keep living your life like that, I mean for God's sake we've got a *baby* coming!" she said, pointing to her stomach dramatically.

I could tell there was nothing I could say that was gonna make her understand the danger Stacy posed to us and our baby, if she kept asking the wrong questions. We may have come through the storm of what I did to her ex-dope boy and her ex-husband, but she was determined that I needed to leave that part of my life behind me.

"You're right, babe, and I apologize. I'm still a work in progress, but I promise you every decision I make will be about giving you and our children the best life possible," I said, pulling her into my arms and kissing her on the forehead.

"Thank you. Can we go in now?" I stepped back and let her lead the way into the building and down the hall to the NA meeting.

We tiptoed inside and found seats in the back, which allowed me to observe everyone present discreetly, including Stacy. I halfway expected her to turn around and look at me from time to time, but she stayed facing forward for the full length of the meeting. I didn't know what she was thinking, but I used the hour to strategize a way to disarm her and pick her brain.

"I'm gonna make rounds and touch base with a few people," Shawndra whispered, after the meeting had come to a close.

"Okay, baby, I'll be here."

Once she was wrapped up in conversation with Angela and another female, I made my way casually over to Stacy, finding her standing alone by the refreshment table.

"Stacy, can I talk to you for a minute?" I asked, as non-threatening as I could.

"About?"

"Well, it's clear your brother's death has affected you greatly, and I understand that on multiple levels. I myself lost a brother recently, and no matter how many people tell me that time heals, I have yet to find the truth in that statement. Being involved in law enforcement for the last twenty years, I've seen my share of senseless violence, but it's worse when it hits home. I don't mean to speak out of turn, but knowing the pain you're in makes me want to help in any way you'll allow," I said, with false sincerity.

"You're a cop?" she asked skeptically, looking me up and down.

"*Was* a cop, and I worked undercover for homicide and narcotics. I'm retired now, though."

"Well, if you're retired, how can you help me?" she asked.

"My job title may have changed, but I'd like to think my skills haven't diminished. You said John was killed on the night I came into town, so I was thinking we could compare what we saw, maybe backtrack through his last day. I know the local police department probably already did that with you, and undoubtedly they're launching a thorough investigation, so—"

"No they're not. They don't give a *damn* about John, because to them he was just another junkie," she said through clenched teeth with barely controlled anger.

I was smiling on the inside, because I'd taken a shot in the dark and hit a bullseye.

"It doesn't matter what mistakes your brother made in his life, no one had the right to kill him, and he deserves justice," I replied, lying with a straight face.

"Do-do you really mean that?" she asked, looking at me completely different now.

"I do," I said, putting a comforting hand on her shoulder, and looking deeply into her pale green eyes.

I watched the emotion swim through the windows to her soul, noticing gratefulness slide into the place where suspicion had existed, when it came to me. Like any unsuspecting fish, she'd swallowed the hook, and now all I had to do was pull on the line.

"How about we exchange numbers and whenever you're ready, we can meet up and put our heads together," I said, pulling my phone out and turning it on.

"Are you sure? I mean, I imagine you want to enjoy your retirement and—"

"Stacy, I wouldn't have offered if I wasn't sincere about righting this wrong," I said, passing her my phone.

The smile she gave me was definitely one of flirtation, but she quickly hid it as she punched her number into my phone and hit send. Once her phone rang, she gave me mine back and not a moment too soon, because I could see Shawndra headed in our direction.

"Call or text whenever, even if you just need someone to talk to who understands what you're going through," I said, swiftly putting my phone back in my pocket just as Shawndra arrived.

"What's going on?" Shawndra asked, looking back and forth between us.

"I was just getting to know your friend. He's a good guy," Stacy, said smiling.

"Oh, I know, he is my *boy*friend after all," Shawndra replied, smoothly hooking her arm through mine to make sure Stacy caught all the shade she was throwing.

"I'm glad we had a chance to chat, and I'm sorry for how I came at you earlier," Stacy said, extending her hand to me.

Once I shook, it she smiled at us before walking away.

"Okay, what the fuck was *that*?" Shawndra asked, clearly thrown by Stacy's temperature shift.

"What do you mean, babe? I just had a simple conversation with the lass."

"Don't give me that simple conversation bullshit, she smiled at you like she was ready to ride your fucking face," Shawndra whispered, emphatically.

"You know you're exaggerating, so stop it and let's go," I replied, fighting the laughter trying to bubble up out of my throat, while leading her outside to the car.

"Do you wanna go out to eat?" I asked, once I was in the driver's seat.

"I want you to tell me what the fuck you said to Stacy to make her want to get on her knees and suck your dick, because that's damn sure how she was looking at you."

"Where do you *get* this shit from?" I asked, laughing.

"She called you my friend, *my friend*, when she goddamn well heard me when I introduced you as my man. Women who do shit like that are basically saying they wanna fall on your dick. You know it, I know it, so tell me what you two talked about," she demanded.

It was obvious she wasn't letting this go, because she had some other shit on her mind, and I needed to put that to bed immediately. After starting the car and getting us on the move, I replayed my conversation with Stacy, making sure to leave nothing out. By the time we'd made it through the Culver's Restaurant drive-thru, Shawndra knew the whole story and was silently chewing on it, along with her buffalo chicken tenders and cheese curds.

"Do you remember how we used to talk about you writing books when you were locked up?" she asked, suddenly.

"Yeah," I replied, slowly, wondering where that question had come from.

"Well, I think you really need to consider it some more, because you tell some really believable stories. I mean, no wonder she was looking at you like you were her fucking hero, you sold her one *hell* of a dream."

"I was just trying to get her to stop looking at me with the side eye, and I thought taking a different approach would make you happy," I replied.

"Sure, I *love* that this bitch wants to fuck you instead of fingering you to the cops," she said, sarcastically.

I knew how jealous Shawndra could be, and I didn't see this conversation getting any better, so I did the smart thing and kept my mouth shut.

When we got home, I put on a romantic comedy and rubbed Shawndra's feet, while we spent some quality couple time together. By the time the movie was over, and the good guy got the girl, my own lady was barely able to keep her eyes open. Like the gentleman I was, I helped her to bed and tucked her in, with a promise to join her after I'd called Maleah back to tell her the good news. When I'd turned my phone on to exchange numbers with Stacy, I'd noticed that I had ten new voicemails, and I had no doubt that every last one was from Su'Ryah. Knowing the drama that awaited, I chose to step outside to make my call, but when I got out front and pulled my phone out, I found a text from Stacy. It was innocent enough, because it only asked was I still awake, but to be asking that question at one o'clock in the morning signaled bad intentions. I responded that I was awake and had in fact just put Shawndra to bed, and before I could block she'd replied with a question of could we meet up and talk.

She had no idea that she was courting her own death, and the gentlemen in me wouldn't allow me to tell her. Instead, I asked her when and where we should meet. To my supreme delight, she sent me her home address, which I immediately tapped into my phone's GPS. I sent her a text telling her I would be there as soon I could, and then I went to look in on Shawndra. She was sleeping so beautifully and peacefully that I dared not wake her. At least, that was the justification I used to slither off into the night with the intentions of sinning in more ways than one. Forty-five minutes later, I knocked on Stacy's apartment door, and she opened it. Naked.

Chapter 18

"Thanks for coming," she said, seductively walking away from the open door, and making it clear it was my decision to follow or not. As a man, I could appreciate any woman's beauty, but Stacy wasn't exactly my type. Her long brown hair flowed down her back to her small waist, and she had a nice little ass to fit her slender frame. Her breasts were obviously bought and paid for, but I needed a woman who had meat on her bones and could take *dick* when called upon. I needed the woman I'd left at home sleeping, and despite my previous indiscretions, I wouldn't be laying down in another woman's bed tonight. I would be laying her to rest though.

I stepped inside her apartment, making sure to lock the door behind me, before following her down the hall into the living room. I immediately noticed the candles burning around the room as the smell of vanilla moved through the air, knowing this must be her attempt at setting the mood.

"So, Stacy, why am I here?" I asked, taking a seat on the opposite side of the couch from her.

"I just needed someone to talk to. You made me feel more comfortable than anyone has in a long time."

"I can tell you're comfortable," I replied, looking her up and down.

She didn't blush. Instead, she smiled the same way I imagined a spider would when she saw dinner stuck in her web.

"I'm not ashamed of my body, and I *am* in my own home behind closed doors, so there's really no need for clothes. Besides, I know my body looks better than Shawndra's."

ARYANNA

She probably thought my smile was because I was agreeing with the statement she'd just made, but I was really smiling because she'd erased all doubt about me killing her.

"I thought Shawndra was your friend," I said, neutrally.

"Friends? No, she walked past my brother and I like we didn't exist on most days, and on the days she actually spoke, it was always done from a place of superiority. Even though she was a junkie just like us, she felt like she was better because she never had to do the *really* ugly shit to get her fix. That don't mean she's better, it just means nobody probably wanted to pay for sex. My brother was infatuated with her for a little while, but she didn't look at him twice, which makes her an uppity bitch in my book. So are we friends? If we were, would I be getting ready to fuck her *boy*friend like he was my own?" she asked, scooting closer to me on the couch until we were breathing the same air.

"So, you're gonna fuck me? That's why I'm here?"

"Of course it is, you knew that when you accepted my invitation to come over in the middle of the night. Before we get to the grand finale, let's take it from the top. I'm gonna show you the benefits of having to suck dick to support your habit," she said, reaching for my zipper. I wanted to simply break her neck right now, but that would've been way too suspicious, considering how her brother died. I had to play my hand and wait on my moment.

"Just relax, baby, you're in good hands now," she whispered, pulling my dick out and quickly wrapping her lips around it.

I was a man committed to not fucking this woman, but I was still *a man*, and there was no way to stop my dick from rising to the occasion under the powerful suction she was putting down. If I didn't think of something fast, this situation was gonna get all the way out of control.

170

"St-Stacy hold up, I gotta use the bathroom."

"Go ahead, I'll swallow that too," she replied, going right back to deep throating my dick.

"As-as freaky as that sounds, I do pl-plan to kiss you at some point. I'll only take a minute," I protested, literally trying to run from her mouth.

"Hurry up, I want you to put that big black dick in every hole I've got," she said, pulling back reluctantly.

"Where's the bathroom?"

"Down the hall, first door on the right," she said, laying back on the couch, spreading her legs wide open, and slowly pushing three fingers inside her pussy. Under the glow of the candlelight, I saw something in between her legs that could make this night go a lot smoother, but first I needed to go to the bathroom. Once I was behind the door with it locked, I wasted no time carefully going through her medicine cabinet in search of what I needed. I was almost convinced that she was hiding it somewhere else in the apartment, but when I looked under the bathroom sink, I hit the jackpot. I quickly took what I needed and put it in my pocket, flushed the toilet, and made my way back to the living room where I found her moments away from finding her first orgasm.

"Let me help you with that," I said, moving swiftly to the couch and kneeling in front of her.

"I want you-you inside me," she panted.

"Patience, sweetheart, I wanna taste you first."

My declaration made her eagerly reach for my head, so she could pull me into her land of mystery, but I smacked her hands away and positioned her just how I wanted her. I started out with kisses up her inner thighs, careful to avoid the fresh track marks I encountered along the way, while my fingers took a walk through the gates of her ecstasy. Within seconds, I had her speaking in tongues like an ancient prophet, her head trashing from side to side as the temperature of her inferno continued to rise.

"Your-your mouth, please," she begged, as her pussy gripped my fingers tighter than a handshake.

I bit her thigh just to test the water, and her response was the vocal sign of pleasure I'd anticipated. The time had come to seize the moment. I swiftly pulled my fingers out of her and gave her what she asked for, licking her pussy slow and steady like she was my favorite ice cream. Her breath came in ragged gasps, telling me that she wasn't far from having her world tilted by a massive climactic shift, which meant I had to hurry. Without interrupting the spell I was weaving with my tongue, I slowly pulled her syringe from my pocket, and filled it with air. With that done, I used one hand to push her legs wide open and I went to work on giving her that long goodnight. When my lips locked around her slit, the flood gates opened and her long-awaited downpour was unleashed, along with her echoing screams of complete satisfaction. Knowing that she wouldn't feel anything except euphoria, I waited until she was at the height of her orgasm, before slipping the needle into one of her track marks and pushing the plunger until she had a full dose of silent death.

"You want this dick now?" I asked, sweetly.

"Oh yes, daddy, give-give-give…"

Suddenly, the look on her face transformed from glorious bliss to utter confusion and then, her stare just went blank as the rise and fall of her chest came to an abrupt halt. After waiting a full two minutes to make sure the miracle of life didn't return, I went about the business of setting the scene. I went back to the bathroom and got her kit that contained all her drugs and paraphernalia, making sure to wipe everything down I'd touched so I didn't leave my prints behind. After finding her phone and erasing our messages, it took me ten minutes to load her body with a lethal dose of meth, wipe everything down again, and slip quickly from her apartment as if I'd never been there.

I used the drive back to Shawndra's to clear my mind of everything except what had just happened, and I replayed it over and over again, looking for any potential mistakes I might've made. By the time I'd made it to the Quick Stop gas station, I was confident that I'd sufficiently covered my tracks, except for one last thing. I quickly wiped my phone of all texts and messages, even those from Su'Ryah. I filled my gas tank, bought what I needed out of the store, and then continued my journey home. I had no doubt that once Stacy's death became public knowledge, Shawndra wouldn't suspect me of having anything to do with it, but as I pulled into the driveway and saw her sitting out front, I knew I had some explaining to do in my immediate future.

"What are you doing up, babe?" I asked, approaching her with concern, instead of the transparent guilt I was feeling.

"I woke up and you weren't next to me, so I went looking for you. Imagine my surprise to not find you anywhere in the house, so where were you?"

"I wasn't tired after talking to your stepdaughter, so I figured I'd go out and pick up some stuff you needed," I replied, passing her the bag I'd been holding.

When she looked inside she couldn't keep the smile off of her face, and that made me breathe a whole lot easier.

"You got me Mountain Dew and Lucky Charms."

"Yep, I saw you were out of both, and since you can't smoke, I figured I better have everything else you needed in order to keep you from blowing my shit back," I said, smiling at her convincingly.

"You made a good decision. Now, come on so I can reward you," she replied, holding her hand out to me.

With a sigh of relief, I took it and followed her in the house, but I knew I wasn't out of the weeds yet.

"Why don't you put that stuff away and meet me downstairs?" I suggested, smacking her playfully on the ass.

"Ow! Not so hard."

I laughed at her response, but as soon as she turned her head I vaulted down the stairs and went straight for the bathroom. The first thing I did was fill my mouth with Listerine to get the taste of Stacy off of my tongue, and once that was done I washed my face with soap.

"Babe?" Shawndra called, from right outside the bathroom door.

"It's open."

"You must not be using the toilet then, because you *never* leave the door unlocked," she replied, laughing as she pushed the door open.

I quickly rinsed my face before drying it and going to her.

"You're *so* funny," I said, picking her up and carrying her into the bedroom, where I tossed her on her bed.

The laughter quickly died in her throat when I started peeling my clothes off, and by the time I was standing unabashedly naked at the foot of her bed, all I could hear was her fast breathing.

"Let me do that," I said, when she began undressing herself. I climbed on the bed and helped her wiggle out of her capri's and panties, before pulling her tank top over her head and tossing it aside with the rest of her clothes.

"You're always more beautiful than the last time I saw you," I whispered, leaning down to kiss her tenderly.

She opened her mouth and legs to me in one fluid motion, allowing me to push my way inside her as our tongues began the familiar dance of seduction. The tightness of her pussy and the way it literally sucked me in always took my breath away, but the emotional connection created in these moments was my CPR. Even without music, I could hear our love song playing with each moan that came from deep in her throat, forcing me to dive into her with increasing need. The feeling of her teeth sinking into my bottom lip sent a bolt of lightning up my spine that resulted in me delivering pounding blows, which had her holding onto me tightly. Each stroke given and passionate kiss exchanged, brought my soul closer to hers and made me realize how much I truly loved this woman.

"I-need-you," she professed, locking her legs around my waist, and forcing me to sample the water at the bottom of her well.

"Show me," I demanded, increasing the pace of my strokes to make her cum for me.

When her tsunami rolled in, it took all of my willpower not to cum with her, but I was determined to make her a slave to my love tonight.

"Lay on your side," I ordered, just as the aftershocks of her orgasm began to rock her body.

She quickly did as instructed, figuring I would spoon feed her this dick, but I had other plans. I stayed exactly as I was after she'd turned on her right side, pulling her right leg out so I was straddling it, while pushing her left leg towards her stomach. Once I had her positioned just right, I slid back inside her slowly, while guiding her hand in between her legs.

Let's do this together," I whispered in her ear.

Past experience taught me that playing with her clit while I was deep inside her would send her into the next stratosphere, and that was my goal. A short five minutes later, I could feel her body coming to life, but right before she reached the end of the earth, I rolled her onto her stomach and molded our two bodies into one. My jackhammer strokes were enough to snap any sane thought we possessed, causing us both to climax loud enough to wake everyone within a square mile. As badly as I didn't want to hurt her or our child, I was incapable of rolling off of her until my body stopped shaking and she released me from inside her walls.

"You-you always do that," I panted, weakly.

"Do what?"

"Try to pussy whip me by putting the clamps on my dick," I replied, chuckling and sucking in much needed oxygen.

"Stop trying to ram your dick through me then! Be gentle or I'll have to bend you to my will."

"Yeah right, you ain't built like that," I said, arrogantly.

"We'll see about that," she replied, taking ahold of my dick as she curled up next to me, and laid her head on my chest.

We fell asleep just like that, both of us smiling.

Chapter 19

I awoke to the feeling of someone shaking me roughly, snatching me from my peaceful dream land and thrusting me into full penitentiary alertness.

"What-what is it?" I asked, scrambling out of bed, looking around wide-eyed for the nearest threat.

"We need to talk."

"Talk? Shawndra I *know* you didn't just wake me up because you wanted to *talk*," I said, blinking to get my eyes to adjust to the late morning sunlight.

"Yes, I did, because it's important. I need to ask you something, and don't bullshit me, Delontae. Where did you go last night?"

"Are you fucking with me right now? Didn't we already have this conversation when I came back and graced you with the shit you needed?"

"Yes, we did, but what I need now is for you to look me in the eye and tell me that you didn't kill her," she replied, moving to stand right in front of me.

"Kill who?"

For a moment, she simply stared at me and I knew her Spidey sense was tingling, which meant I had to keep a straight face at all costs.

"Baby, kill *who*?" I asked, taking her face in both of my hands and staring her straight in the eyes.

"Stacy's dead," she replied, watching me closely.

"Stacy? Oh shit, now I see why you'd ask me," I said, taking a step back and dropping my hands to my side.

"Delontae, did you—"

"No, baby, I didn't. I don't know how she died or where, but it wasn't by my hand."

"She died at her house from an apparent overdose," she said, sadly.

"We ran out of dope a long time ago. Furthermore, I didn't know this girl well enough to know where she lived, so why would you ask me if I did it?"

"I just needed you to look me in the eyes, because I knew last night you felt like she was a problem and—"

"And you convinced me that I need to handle our problems a different way," I said, pulling her against me and kissing her until I was sure all thoughts of Stacy had left her brain.

"Take a shower with me," I insisted, kissing her neck.

"I c-can't, babe, I've gotta go pick out my gun."

"Your carry conceal license came through?" I asked, looking at her quickly.

"Yep! See, I *do* listen to you when it comes to important things, so remember this moment," she replied, poking me in the chest.

Her being licensed to carry a pistol was the compromise we'd made because she didn't want me riding around with a gun, let alone a *dirty* gun. I understood her logic, but being without a weapon within reach wasn't how I could live my life at this moment, and now I wouldn't have to.

"You're right, you did listen, and I'm proud of you. That don't mean you can pick out no punk-ass gun though, you better get something that's gonna put a nigga down before you even start shooting," I said.

"That doesn't make any sense."

"Baby, you say that because you ain't never been on the business end of a hand cannon. I promise you when one is pulled on you, you're gonna get low, run, hide, *all* that shit," I replied, laughing despite being serious.

"You're *crazy*! If you want to go gun shopping with me, you better hurry up and get your ass in the shower. You know James has an early game today."

I tried to lean in and kiss her again with hopes of persuading her to join me in the shower, but she avoided my lips and backed away from me.

"Go shower now!" she said, laughing and pointing.

I could tell I was fighting a losing battle, so I gave up and did as I was told. Under the spray of the hot water is where I actually took a deep breath, because I'd sufficiently convinced Shawndra that the timing of Stacy's death was simply coincidence. There was no doubt in my mind of whether or not she could handle the truth, or be trusted with it, but I lied because I didn't want to disappoint her. I wanted to be the man she knew I was capable of being, because that was the only way our future didn't end with more visits separated by glass, or her putting flowers on my grave. I wanted my kids to look up to me, which meant I had to be around for that to happen.

Deep down, I knew I had to change, but the reality right now was that life was continuing to happen around me. I could only roll with the punches. Ten minutes later, I stepped out of the shower and went back into the bedroom to dry off, where I found Shawndra sitting on the bed. With my phone to her ear.

"Hold on, you can ask him who I am," Shawndra said, tossing me my phone and crossing her arms over her chest.

Her resting bitch face was on full-tilt hoodie, which told me exactly who was on the phone before I put it to my war.

"Hello?"

"Delontae, what bitch you got answering your motherfucking phone? And how the fuck you gonna play me like that?" Su'Ryah yelled.

"First of all, remember who you're talking to because right now, you're trippin' and—"

"*Trippin'*! Nigga, you ain't begun to see me trip, but you 'bout to if you don't tell me who that bitch was that answered your goddamn phone!"

All traces of the calm, cool, collected, polished Doctor Su'Ryah Davenport were long gone, and it was obvious that I was now dealing with the girl from the same mud as me. If that wasn't enough of a task to handle, the look Shawndra was leveling at me told me death was around the next corner.

"Su'Ryah, I really don't have time to argue with you, so either check your tone or you'll be talking to yourself. Now, what do you—"

"Your ass better *not* walk out of this damn room, Delontae, because if you do you better not stop until you're out of Wisconsin," Shawndra warned.

"Oh, so you're in Wisconsin," Su'Ryah said, immediately.

"No, I'm not in Wisconsin," I replied, stopping in my tracks.

My move had been second nature and pure instinct to put some space between me and the very angry women in front of me, but it was obvious she wasn't having it.

"Yes bitch, he is in Madison, Wisconsin, with his *wife*, so stay in your lane, *Doctor*!" Shawndra yelled, hopping up off the bed and moving towards me.

"Wife?" Su'Ryah screamed in my ear.

There was no way to fight these two battles at the same time, so I did the only thing I could do and hung up the phone, giving my undivided attention to the woman with flames in her eyes.

"Tell me again how you *didn't* fuck that bitch," Shawndra said, angrily.

The look on her face and the tone of her voice told me that neither half-truths, nor bold-face lies, would fix this situation. It was obvious the time had come to keep shit one hundred.

"Baby, listen—"

"Don't *touch* me," she said, putting her hands up and backing away from me.

That made it clear that trying to sweet talk her and entice her with my nakedness wasn't gonna work either. My ringing phone only added to the tension growing between us, but I fixed that by throwing it at the wall and shattering it.

"Really," Shawndra said, shaking her head.

I didn't say anything. Instead, I chose to get dressed with hopes that it would give both of us a needed moment to calm down, so we could talk without yelling. To her credit, Shawndra sat on the bed and waited, demonstrating more patience than I would've been able to if the roles were reversed. Once I was dressed, I sat beside her and tried to find the right words to use.

"I lied and I apologize for that. I won't give you bullshit excuses, because it doesn't matter why I lied about sleeping with Su'Ryah, the only thing that matters is that I lied. Our professional relationship turned into something neither of us saw coming, but at the end of the day I'm here with *you*, I'm having a baby with *you*, and I'm building a family with *you*," I said, sincerely.

"I understand that, but would you be here with me if shit hadn't gone sideways for you in D.C.?"

"Baby, I was always meant to be with you. Don't you know that by now?" I asked, turning to look at her.

"I mean, I thought I did, but I told you while you were still locked up that I didn't wanna deal with random bitches from your past, still trying to fall on the dick. I don't have time for that drama, and I'm a good woman who deserves better than that. I told you before I won't put up with that cheating shit."

"You'll never have to, baby, I promise," I replied, taking her hand in mine and moving to kneel in front of her.

"I'm yours, Shawndra, to have and to hold, in sickness and in health, in good times and bad, for richer or for poorer, for as long as we both shall live."

Did you just recite your vows to me?" she asked, unable to stop the smile that was now lighting up her face.

"I did, I do, and I will again in front of the world."

I could see she was still trying to be upset with me, but she knew I loved her and wanted her above all else.

"You better tell that bitch it's over, Delontae, and I mean it. I can understand Maleah wanting to have a relationship with her, but you don't need to have anything else to do with her. Right?"

"You're absolutely right," I replied quickly, kissing her before she could change her mind.

"And don't think you're getting any make-up sex right now, you know we've gotta go," she said, pushing me back and standing up.

I followed her lead, making sure to give her my car keys without her having to ask, which made her laugh and nod her hand in approval. The gun store was only a fifteen-minute drive from the house, but once we got there, I had to spend another half-hour talking her out of getting a pink camouflage Glock .40. To her it was just the cutest thing, but to me it was "no, no thank you, not gonna happen, nope, and stop playing." All rolled into one. Finally; we agreed on the standard black Glock .27, two different holsters, a portable gun safe, a few extra clips, and a lot of extra ammo so she could learn how to shoot.

With that task completed, we stopped at the Verizon store to get me a new phone, and then we went straight across town to James's baseball game. In truth, his team wasn't all that good, but I wouldn't miss a game because I knew he wanted me there. Ever since my heart to heart with William, we'd been spending more time with the kids on a regular basis, and there was never a problem getting them for the weekend. The joy of having them in my life was something I couldn't put into words, but I made sure they understand how much they meant to me every chance I got.

"It's only the bottom of the first inning so we didn't miss much," I said, sitting with Shawndra in the bleachers behind home plate.

"Yeah, well we would've been on time if you would've let me buy what I wanted."

I chose to ignore her comment while searching for James in the dugout.

"He's coming up to bat," I said, pointing towards the warm-up area where he was taking practice swings.

"Yeah, and there's his dad, Lisa, and Marie over there," Shawndra replied, nodding towards the bleachers that were angled to the left of us.

"Are we gonna tell the kids about the new baby?"

"Why not, that'll give them plenty of time to get used to the idea," she replied, taking my hand in hers and smiling at me.

I'd heard before that introducing a new baby into a household could cause major sibling rivalry, and constant fights for attention, but I knew Marie and James would love their new brother or sister.

"Come on, James. Let's go, buddy!" I yelled, when I saw him making his way to home plate.

He immediately locked in on my voice and spotted us sitting a few feet away. I could tell his smile was one of relief and joy, and that warmed my heart. Even when he ended up striking out, his smile never faltered. We stayed for the entire game, yelling until our voices cracked, but neither of us minded because these were the moments we'd envisioned for us. When the game was over, James ran off the field straight to us and threw himself into our open arms.

"I thought you might not come," he said.

"Blame your mom for us being late," I replied, immediately.

"Oh, what*ever!*" Shawndra said, laughing and sticking her tongue out at me.

Suddenly, our group hug got bigger as Marie pushed her way in.

"What took you so long to get over here?" I asked, hugging her tightly.

"I don't know, my legs are short, I guess," she replied, smiling up at me with that one dimple in her cheek.

I could see William and Lisa coming towards us, and the petty in me kicked in.

"We've got a surprise for you," I announced, locking eyes with Shawndra.

"What is it, what is it?" James asked, insistently.

"It's not a video game," I warned, knowing how his mind worked.

"No it's not, it's *much* better than that," Shawndra said, pausing dramatically.

"*What,* Mom?" Marie asked, impatiently.

"We're gonna have a baby," Shawndra whispered.

"A baby," they both yelled excitedly, jumping up and down.

I knew William and his wife might've been too far away to hear everything, but the ill look that came over his wife's face told me she'd heard something. Shawndra had told me that they'd been trying to have a baby, unsuccessfully up to this point, so our happy news was sure to make them feel some type of way.

"William, Lisa, how are you?" I asked, smiling widely.

"Shawndra, De-Delontae," William replied, neutrally.

"Dad, Mom's gonna have a baby!" James said, joyfully.

"Con-congratulations," William said, avoiding eye contact with both me and Shawndra.

His wife, on the other hand, was openly staring at Shawndra, and she was damn near green with jealously.

"Hey guys, we'll celebrate this weekend, okay? I'm sure your dad wants to take you out for ice cream now," I said, hugging them again.

"Okay, but you have to take care of my mom," James insisted.

"Yeah," Marie chimed in.

"I will, I promise. We'll pick you up in a couple days," I assured them.

After giving Shawndra another hug, they left us standing there holding hands.

"You really *are* the king of petty," Shawndra said, laughing.

"Only when it's deserved or when it's fun. Come on, let's go."

I used the time riding shotgun on the way home to activate my new phone and set it up, wondering why I hadn't gotten another phone before now. I logged onto my Facebook page to send Maleah a message with my new number, and explicit instructions not to give it to Su'Ryah, but I found a surprise waiting for me.

"Oh shit," I mumbled.

"What's wrong now?"

"I've got thirty-six messages from Maleah," I replied, opening the first one.

"What do they say?"

"All of them say I need to call her ASAP and I think we both know what it's about."

Shawndra looked over at me, but she didn't say anything before turning her eyes back to the road. I know there was no way to avoid my daughter, so I dialed the number she'd left for me, and waited to take my tongue lashing.

"Maleah, it's me," I said, once she picked up.

"Dad, what the fuck is going on?"

"It's a long story, but—"

"Dad, listen to me. Whatever you did, you need to fix it because Su'Ryah has lost her damn mind!"

"Why do you say that, what happened?" I asked, already dreading the answer.

"She took a fucking baseball bat to everything in the house. I mean, literally broke everything that could be broken."

"Where is she?" I asked.

"That's the thing, I have no fucking idea."

Chapter 20

Two days later

"Can I make you breakfast?" I asked, kissing along her neck and across the top of her back gently.

"Of course you can, you can do anything you want for me, after what you just did *to* me."

"I can do it again if you like," I whispered, wrapping my arms around her tighter, and moving my hips to remind her that my dick was still deep inside her.

"Okay, but can you feed me first so my sugar level doesn't bottom out while I'm riding you?"

As badly as I now wanted to skip breakfast so we could live off of the nourishment of each other, I knew diabetes wasn't nothing to play with, especially for a pregnant woman.

"I got you, babe," I said, kissing her shoulder one more time before climbing out of her and the bed.

"Nice ass," she commented.

"Ditto," I replied, looking at her beautiful body again, before making my way to the kitchen. Once I found a serving tray big enough to accommodate two bowls, I poured us each a bowl of Lucky Charms, and set the half-gallon of milk between them. I took a red rose from the vase in the kitchen windowsill, clipped it, and added it to the tray too. The finishing touches came in the form of two spoons, and then I was on my way back downstairs.

"Breakfast is..." my voice trailed off when I realized I was talking to an empty bed.

"Are you just gonna keep showing me your ass?" she asked from behind me, smacking me on it.

"That wasn't my intent, I expected you to be still holding the bed in recovery from our morning workout."

"I had to check my sugar or you would've been up my ass about that," she replied, moving around me and going back to the bed to sit down.

"Up your ass, huh?" I said, smiling devilishly.

"Don't even think about it, I told you my ass is for *exit only*. Now bring me my food please."

"Oh, I'll get my dick in there eventually, I'm patient and determined," I replied, laughing and sitting the tray in front of her.

I loved that the first thing she grabbed was the rose, and she smiled while putting it to her nose and looking at me.

"I love you too," I said, even though she hadn't spoken the words out loud.

One of the best things about our relationship was the chemistry we shared. A lot of people could be in sync when it came to bedroom activities, but completely clueless to each other's wants, needs, and desires outside of orgasmic pleasure. Shawndra and I shared the rare chemistry that translated outside the bedroom and spilled over into everyday life. I knew what she thought and felt without her having to tell me. Sometimes she'd simply make a sound and I would know what she wanted. Maybe it came from the fact that the first few years of our friendship and relationship developed without the benefit of normal physical interaction. Maybe the simpler answer was that she was the counterpart God had made for me. All I knew for sure was that what she and I shared, I'd never known with another woman, not even with Su'Ryah. I appreciated it more every day we spent together.

"The kids sent me a text already," she said, putting the rose down and pouring milk in both of our cereal bowls.

"Wondering when we're coming to get them," I guessed, smiling because it was the same routine every time it was their weekend to be with us.

We were *definitely* the cool parents.

"Of course, and James wants to know if you'll get tickets for the Brewers baseball game this weekend."

"Who are they playing?" I asked, around a mouthful of cereal.

"The Cubs I think, but it's a home game. I told him that he could ask you when we picked them up in an hour," she replied, sheepishly.

I could only laugh because she always caved quick when the kids started sending text messages for us to come pick them up earlier than planned. I didn't mind though, because I genuinely enjoyed spending time with them. Marie spent uninterrupted hours on the computer playing her games, but James was the biggest Wisconsin sports fan in the world, and wanted to go to any game he could.

"If we're picking them up in an hour, you better hurry and eat because we still have to shower, *and* I'm getting some more of your loving before we go," I declared, smiling at her.

"We don't have enough time for all of that."

The look I leveled at her was one of determination, but it only made her smile wider.

"You'll be okay until later, so stop looking at me like you're pussy starved. Hurry up and eat."

I did like I was told, figuring I'd literally have her back against the wall once we were in the shower, but twenty minutes later, I'd only succeeded in getting a hand job. In her defense though, it was a world-class hand job.

"Hurry up and get dressed, I'll get the car," I said, after putting on a sweat suit and my Air Max.

"I'll be there in a minute," she called from the bedroom closet.

I grabbed the keys, went upstairs, opened the door, and stopped in my tracks as the impossible became possible in front of my very eyes.

"What the fuck-how did you-where did you come from?" I stammered, fighting against my own disbelief.

"I told you before that I come from Southeast D.C., just like you, weren't you listening?" Su'Ryah asked, smiling sweetly.

"You know what I mean, Su'Ryah, how the fuck did you find me?" I asked, looking past her to see if she had any other surprises with her, like my daughter.

"Oh, well that's a long story, and I'm tired from my travels so aren't you gonna invite me in?"

That question along told me this bitch had lost her *entire* mind because if she'd found me here, then she knew exactly who lived here.

"Invite you in? You can't be serious," I replied.

"I'm dead serious."

Her words were laced with determination, and the eyes I'd once found so beautiful and hypnotizing were telegraphing the same message. Neither made the hair on the back of my neck stand up though. That only happened because of the metal clicking sound I heard coming from her purse. I was all too familiar with that noise, and I knew exactly what caused it.

"Come in," I said, backing away from the door slowly, making sure to keep my hands where she could see them.

"Thank you. Now where's your friend, Shawndra?" She asked, looking around expectantly.

"Whatever this is, it's between us, Su'Ryah, and no one else."

"That's only true if you're not fucking this bitch, and before you open your mouth to say you're not, I'll tell you now that your word don't mean shit. I want to hear it from her mouth, and look her in the eyes. So where is she?" Su'Ryah asked again.

"Listen, it's not even like—"

The sight of her pulling the chrome .357 revolver out of her bag froze my words, because it was obvious she meant business. All I could think about was protecting Shawndra and our baby, which meant I had to buy time.

"You don't need that. Come on," I said, turning and leading the way downstairs.

As soon as I reached the bottom step, Shawndra was coming out of the bedroom.

"You didn't have to come back for me, I told you I would- who's that?" she asked, stopping a few feet away, looking from me to Su'Ryah and back to me.

"I was wondering the same thing about you a couple days ago because as far as I knew, *I* was his future wife," Su'Ryah said, stopping next to me at the bottom of the stairs.

I could tell by the look on Shawndra's face that she recognized Su'Ryah's voice, but the sight of the pistol she was holding forced her to remain calm. For now.

"Why is she here?" Shawndra asked.

"I'm here for answers, so why don't we all take a seat on the couch over there," Su'Ryah replied, gesturing with the gun in a reckless way that had my heart beating faster.

I nodded slightly towards Shawndra and she backed up slowly, until her knees came in contact, with the couch forcing her to sit down. I was going for the seat next to her, but then thought better of it, because to appear undecided would play towards Su'Ryah feelings, and hopefully keep her calm. Instead, I sat in the chair that was in between the couch and the loveseat.

"Why don't you make the formal introductions, Delontae," Su'Ryah suggested, taking a seat across from Shawndra.

"Su'Ryah this is Shawndra, Shawndra this is Su'Ryah."

Both women stared at each other, sizing up the competition like two prize fighters ready to do battle,

"I would say nice to meet you, but I'd much rather skip the bullshit and get right down to the reason I'm here. Are you fucking Delontae?" Su'Ryah asked.

"Like I told you on the phone, I'm his *wife*, so yes, I'm fucking him," Shawndra replied, candidly.

I immediately noticed Su'Ryah's grip on the pistol tighten, which caused me to flinch because I had no intention of letting her shoot Shawndra.

"His wife, huh? That's funny because I didn't find any record of a marriage license issued to you two, and I did a *thorough* search," Su'Ryah said.

"How did you even find out about her?" I asked, trying to shift the focus onto me.

"It took some digging, considering she wasn't mentioned anywhere in your prison paperwork, or prior to that. I'm sure you were counting on that considering your current legal entanglements, and it's obviously been a safe bet, since the cops haven't tracked you down way out here. I was smarter than them though, so I called in some favors and had your visitation records pulled. You only had one visitor from the cheese head state, and that was little Shawndra Marie Fry here. From there, all it took was a couple tanks of gas and a one-track mind, and now here we are getting to know each other. Do you know him, Shawndra, I mean *really* know him?" she asked.

"I wouldn't call him my husband if I didn't know him, and make no mistake, he *is* my husband," Shawndra replied, emphatically.

"Whatever you say, I'm sure he'll fit right in with your upper middle class family perfectly. At least Delontae will, but 'The Lion' probably won't be invited to the family reunion," Su'Ryah replied, smiling.

"I'm not worried about 'The Lion', I know what to do to make him sit," Shawndra said, smiling too.

Her comment erased Su'Ryah's smile with a quickness and caused her hand to tighten on her gun again. I shot Shawndra a look that begged her not to provoke the crazy doctor, because it was becoming increasingly obvious that she'd drank the kook-aid.

"That's cute, Shawndra, but knowing his nickname doesn't mean you actually know him, or have seen what he's capable of. For example, I'd almost bet my life he didn't tell you what happened when he came back to D.C. to help his daughter get out of trouble. I'm not talking about the way I came all over the dick you're claiming as yours only, I'm actually referring to the six people he killed, one of which was a sixteen-year-old innocent girl," Su'Ryah stated, maliciously.

I could feel Shawndra's gaze immediately shift my way, but my attention was focused solely on Su'Ryah as all good feelings I had for her slowly started to evaporate. I wouldn't allow myself to feel the pain bubbling up within me for the disappointment and hurt I'd caused Shawndra. Instead, I focused on the growing anger towards this bitch for her pettiness.

"It don't matter what you say or what you tell her, it don't even matter if she leaves me, I still won't be with you," I said, coldly.

I saw her smile falter a little, but the determination still shined brightly in her eyes and with it, just a hint of the madness she'd hidden so well up to this point.

"Delontae, I know you love me because what we have is real and—"

"Had, what we *had* was real. And yes, there was love in those moments, but I'm not in love with you Su'Ryah," I said, truthfully.

"You're not in love with her either, Delontae. I mean, you need to face reality, you'll never fit into her world and she ain't built for yours," Su'Ryah replied.

"You don't know *what* I'm built for, you *don't* know me, and you *damn* sure don't know what we have," Shawndra said, with hostility.

"What you have? Bitch, what you have is cum on your breath and back problems because you can't seem to stay off it, but let's not bullshit like you have anything real, meaningful, or lasting with him because you *don't*," Su'Ryah stated nastily, squeezing the gun so right that I thought she might fire and accidentally shoot it off.

"Are you really that blind or that misinformed? What I have is *years* of getting to know Delontae, becoming his best friend, and holding him down when the world seemed to forget about him. What I have is a bond and a love that can't be broken by some random bitch getting a taste of the dick, because I guarantee you when you tasted it, the scent of my pussy was still fresh on it. What I have is a man who would give me the world if I asked, or burn the motherfucker to the ground to prevent me from being hurt. I admit you're right. I probably do have cum on my breath, but that's not the only place his cum has been either, because the best thing I have is the future you can't give him. I'm pregnant with his child," Shawndra replied passionately, smiling in a way that translated into three simple words. Checkmate, game over. The pride I felt in watching this unusually soft-spoken, shy woman, blow Su'Ryah's shit back superseded my anger, but the fear of Su'Ryah's next move kept my celebration an internal one. My eyes remained glued to Su'Ryah's face, hoping that if she were gonna make any move on Shawndra, it would be telegraphed first. Seconds of silence felt like minutes of agony, but finally it was broken in a way that I never would've anticipated. Su'Ryah began laughing hysterically. This had Shawndra and I exchanging looks of confusion, even though it was becoming even more clear that the doctor was a deep breath away from being unglued. Her laughter wasn't normal, it grew in both volume and intensity, until she was gasping for air and fanning herself with her free hand.

"Is-is she really pregnant, Delontae?" Su'Ryah asked, once she'd regained enough control to speak.

"Yeah, she is."

"And I'm just gonna assume you actually believe her when she says you're the father, so—"

"Bitch, I'm not a hoe!" Shawndra said, jumping to her feet.

Crazy or not, Su'Ryah had quick reflexes, and her gun was leveled at Shawndra's stomach before I could blink.

"Su'Ryah," I said in warning, fighting the urge to jump up my damn self.

"Talk to your *baby mama,* not me, I'm enjoying the festivities," she replied, calmly.

"Shawndra, chill," I demanded, hoping she would reel her emotions in.

After a few moments, she sat back down, but she didn't take her eyes off of Su'Ryah. This showdown needed to end.

"Su'Ryah, what is it you really want?" I asked.

"That should be obvious. I came all this way for you. Because I love you."

"You love me? Is that why you're pointing a gun at the woman who's carrying my child?" I asked.

Surprisingly, she lowered the gun without hesitation.

"Is that better?" Su'Ryah asked.

"Yes, thank you. Listen, I sincerely apologize if I hurt you, because I *never* intended to do that. You deserved better than what I gave you," I replied.

"I don't know about that. My job is to see through varying layers of bullshit on a daily basis, and we both know that I'm good at my job. You're love for me was real, and that means it can't have just disappeared over the last month and a half, no matter how good her pussy is, or the fact that she's pregnant. Could you love us both? Well, that's not impossible, not even for a sociopath like you. I understand now that I can't really ask you to choose, at least not without all the facts. Before we get to that though, I wanna ask Shawndra a question. How do you feel about having a sister wife?" Su'Ryah asked.

For a minute I thought she was joking because there was *no way* she'd be serious, but when she didn't crack a smile, my mind detoured off into the land of threesomes. I had to shake my head to stay focused because I knew what Shawndra was about to say.

"Sister wife? I'm not sharing my husband with you or anybody else, you crazy bitch, you got me fucked up with the neighbor girl," Shawndra replied, her tone leaving no room for negotiation.

"You sure? Well, if that's how you really feel, I guess Delontae has a decision to make, but I think it should be an informed decision," she replied, reaching into her purse.

I had no idea what she was reaching for, but what she pulled out sucked all the oxygen out of the room. When she put it on the table, I locked eyes with Shawndra, knowing that shit had really hit the fan.

"That's not real," Shawndra whispered in denial.

"I didn't come all this way to tell lies that could be easily verified, so please don't insult my intelligence," Su'Ryah replied, smiling.

My mind flashed back to a few days ago when Shawndra had given me her pregnancy test, and how happy I'd been in that moment. Looking at the word "pregnant" in the screen of the test sitting on the table in front of me didn't inspire the same happiness. Somehow, it only added to my guilt and confusion.

"De-Delontae," Shawndra said, weakly, looking at me with her heart in her eyes.

I had no words that would take this pain away or make this situation better. I'd committed the unforgivable sin of getting another woman pregnant, and allowing it to be thrown in the face of the woman I loved most. How did I come back from that?

"So now that you have all of the facts, I think I'll help you make the right decision," Su'Ryah said, pulling her phone from her purse.

My first thought was my daughter.

"Don't call Maleah," I said quickly.

"Oh, I'm not calling her, just hold on. Hi, I'd like to report the whereabouts of a fugitive," she said into the receiver.

Complete shock gripped me, but then a voice in my head convinced me she was bluffing. As if she was reading my mind Su'Ryah turned the phone towards me so I could see she'd really called the cops, and then she put it back to her ear so she could recite Shawndra's address.

"N-no you didn't you triflin' bitch," Shawndra said, with unbearable pain in her voice.

"Oh, but I did, and it gets better. Your truck and his car are both out of commission, which means your choices are simple, Mr. Mathis. You can leave with me now or go back to prison for a long time," Su'Ryah replied, sweetly.

I didn't know what to say. This bitch had left me utterly speechless. I opened my mouth, hoping to find some words to undo what had just been done, and out of the corner of my eye I saw Shawndra pull her pistol from behind her back, taking aim at Su'Ryah.

"Shawndra, no!"

To Be Continued...
Kill Zone 2
Coming Soon

Submission Guideline

Submit the first three chapters of your completed manuscript to ldpsubmissions@gmail.com, subject line: Your book's title. The manuscript must be in a .doc file and sent as an attachment. Document should be in Times New Roman, double spaced and in size 12 font. Also, provide your synopsis and full contact information. If sending multiple submissions, they must each be in a separate email.

Have a story but no way to send it electronically? You can still submit to LDP/Ca$h Presents. Send in the first three chapters, written or typed, of your completed manuscript to:

LDP: Submissions Dept
Po Box 870494
Mesquite, Tx 75187

DO NOT send original manuscript. Must be a duplicate.

Provide your synopsis and a cover letter containing your full contact information.

Thanks for considering LDP and Ca$h Presents.

ARYANNA

KILL ZONE

LIPSTICK KILLAH **III**

CRIME OF PASSION **II**

By **Mimi**

WHAT BAD BITCHES DO **III**

KILL ZONE **II**

By **Aryanna**

THE COST OF LOYALTY **II**

By **Kweli**

SHE FELL IN LOVE WITH A REAL ONE **II**

By **Tamara Butler**

LOVE SHOULDN'T HURT **III**

RENEGADE BOYS **II**

By **Meesha**

CORRUPTED BY A GANGSTA **III**

By **Destiny Skai**

A GANGSTER'S CODE **III**

By **J-Blunt**

KING OF NEW YORK III

By **T.J. Edwards**

CUM FOR ME **IV**

By **Ca$h & Company**

GORILLAS IN THE BAY

De'Kari

THE STREETS ARE CALLING

Duquie Wilson

KINGPIN KILLAZ II

Hood Rich

ARYANNA

STEADY MOBBIN' **III**
Marcellus Allen
SINS OF A HUSTLER
ASAD

Available Now
RESTRAINING ORDER **I & II**
By **CA$H & Coffee**
LOVE KNOWS NO BOUNDARIES **I II & III**
By **Coffee**
RAISED AS A GOON I, II, III & IV
BRED BY THE SLUMS I, II, III
BLAST FOR ME I & II
ROTTEN TO THE CORE I III
By **Ghost**
LAY IT DOWN **I & II**
LAST OF A DYING BREED
BLOOD STAINS OF A SHOTTA I & II
By **Jamaica**
LOYAL TO THE GAME
LOYAL TO THE GAME II
LOYAL TO THE GAME III
By **TJ & Jelissa**
BLOODY COMMAS I & II
SKI MASK CARTEL I II & III
KING OF NEW YORK I II

KILL ZONE

By **T.J. Edwards**

IF LOVING HIM IS WRONG...I & II

LOVE ME EVEN WHEN IT HURTS

By **Jelissa**

WHEN THE STREETS CLAP BACK I & II III

By **Jibril Williams**

A DISTINGUISHED THUG STOLE MY HEART I II & III

LOVE SHOULDN'T HURT I II

RENEGADE BOYS

By **Meesha**

A GANGSTER'S CODE I & II

By **J-Blunt**

PUSH IT TO THE LIMIT

By **Bre' Hayes**

BLOOD OF A BOSS **I, II, III & IV**

By **Askari**

THE STREETS BLEED MURDER **I, II & III**

THE HEART OF A GANGSTA I II& III

By **Jerry Jackson**

CUM FOR ME

CUM FOR ME 2

CUM FOR ME 3

An **LDP Erotica Collaboration**

BRIDE OF A HUSTLA **I II & II**

THE FETTI GIRLS **I, II& III**

CORRUPTED BY A GANGSTA I & II

By **Destiny Skai**

ARYANNA

WHEN A GOOD GIRL GOES BAD

By **Adrienne**

A GANGSTER'S REVENGE **I II III & IV**

THE BOSS MAN'S DAUGHTERS

THE BOSS MAN'S DAUGHTERS II

THE BOSSMAN'S DAUGHTERS III

THE BOSSMAN'S DAUGHTERS IV

THE BOSS MAN'S DAUGHTERS **V**

A SAVAGE LOVE **I & II**

BAE BELONGS TO ME

A HUSTLER'S DECEIT I, II

WHAT BAD BITCHES DO I, II

By **Aryanna**

A KINGPIN'S AMBITON

A KINGPIN'S AMBITION **II**

I MURDER FOR THE DOUGH

By **Ambitious**

TRUE SAVAGE

TRUE SAVAGE II

TRUE SAVAGE **III**

TRUE SAVAGE **IV**

TRUE SAVAGE **V**

By **Chris Green**

A DOPEBOY'S PRAYER

By **Eddie "Wolf" Lee**

THE KING CARTEL **I, II & III**

By **Frank Gresham**

KILL ZONE

THESE NIGGAS AIN'T LOYAL **I, II & III**

By **Nikki Tee**

GANGSTA SHYT **I II &III**

By **CATO**

THE ULTIMATE BETRAYAL

By **Phoenix**

BOSS'N UP **I , II & III**

By **Royal Nicole**

I LOVE YOU TO DEATH

By Destiny J

I RIDE FOR MY HITTA

I STILL RIDE FOR MY HITTA

By **Misty Holt**

LOVE & CHASIN' PAPER

By **Qay Crockett**

TO DIE IN VAIN

By **ASAD**

BROOKLYN HUSTLAZ

By **Boogsy Morina**

BROOKLYN ON LOCK I & II

By **Sonovia**

GANGSTA CITY

By **Teddy Duke**

A DRUG KING AND HIS DIAMOND I & II III

A DOPEMAN'S RICHES

By Nicole Goosby

TRAPHOUSE KING **I II & III**

ARYANNA

KINGPIN KILLAZ
By **Hood Rich**
LIPSTICK KILLAH **I, II**
CRIME OF PASSION
By **Mimi**
STEADY MOBBN' **I, II**
By **Marcellus Allen**
WHO SHOT YA **I, II**
Renta

KILL ZONE

BOOKS BY LDP'S CEO, CA$H

TRUST IN NO MAN

TRUST IN NO MAN 2

TRUST IN NO MAN 3

BONDED BY BLOOD

SHORTY GOT A THUG

THUGS CRY

THUGS CRY 2

THUGS CRY 3

TRUST NO BITCH

TRUST NO BITCH 2

TRUST NO BITCH 3

TIL MY CASKET DROPS

RESTRAINING ORDER

RESTRAINING ORDER 2

IN LOVE WITH A CONVICT

Coming Soon

BONDED BY BLOOD 2

BOW DOWN TO MY GANGSTA

ARYANNA

www.ingramcontent.com/pod-product-compliance
Lightning Source LLC
Chambersburg PA
CBHW070008260626
47159CB00005B/1723